"You got something against cowboys?"

The deep, sexy voice coming from the front steps sent a jolt through Stacie. She dropped the picture to the table, turned in her seat and met an unblinking blue-eyed gaze.

It was him.

She had to admit Josh looked even better up close. He wore a chambray shirt that made his eyes look strikingly blue and a pair of jeans that hugged his long legs. There was no hat, just lots of thick, dark hair brushing his collar.

The glint in his eyes told her he knew she'd put herself in a hole and was desperately searching for a way to shovel out.

"Of course I like cowboys," she said. "Cowboys make the world go 'round."

Josh's smile widened to a grin.

She'd been caught off guard. Startled. Distracted. By his eyes…and his timing.

Why, oh why, hadn't she kept her mouth shut?

D0047534

Dear Reader,

One of the best parts about writing a book is getting to create the characters. In *Claiming the Rancher's Heart,* one of those characters resembles someone who resides right under my own roof. Want to guess who it is?

Josh, the sexy cowboy hero? No.

His ruggedly handsome friend, Seth? No.

I'll give you a hint. Dark hair with streaks of gray.

Josh's banker father? Wrong again.

Give up? The answer is Bert, Josh's blue heeler. Yes, I have my own cattle dog. Like Bert, my sweet Shug is territorial, intelligent and loves to chase birds. Some day he may even catch one of the swallows who enjoy teasing him so much. (I hope not.)

To see a picture of my rambunctious baby, visit my Web site, www.cindykirk.com, and click on the snapshots link...you'll find him there in all his blue heeler glory!

Cindy Kirk

CLAIMING THE RANCHER'S HEART

CINDY KIRK

Silhouette

SPECIAL EDITION®

Published by Silhouette Books

America's Publisher of Contemporary Romance

If you purchased this book without a cover you should be aware
that this book is stolen property. It was reported as "unsold and
destroyed" to the publisher, and neither the author nor the
publisher has received any payment for this "stripped book."

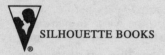

SILHOUETTE BOOKS

ISBN-13: 978-0-373-65444-4
ISBN-10:   0-373-65444-8

Recycling programs
for this product may
not exist in your area.

CLAIMING THE RANCHER'S HEART

Copyright © 2009 by Cynthia Rutledge

All rights reserved. Except for use in any review, the reproduction
or utilization of this work in whole or in part in any form by any
electronic, mechanical or other means, now known or hereafter
invented, including xerography, photocopying and recording, or in
any information storage or retrieval system, is forbidden without
the written permission of the editorial office, Silhouette Books,
233 Broadway, New York, NY 10279 U.S.A.

This is a work of fiction. Names, characters, places and incidents are
either the product of the author's imagination or are used fictitiously, and
any resemblance to actual persons, living or dead, business establishments,
events or locales is entirely coincidental.

This edition published by arrangement with Harlequin Books S.A.

® and TM are trademarks of Harlequin Books S.A., used under license.
Trademarks indicated with ® are registered in the United States Patent
and Trademark Office, the Canadian Trade Marks Office and in other
countries.

Visit Silhouette Books at www.eHarlequin.com

Printed in U.S.A.

Books by Cindy Kirk

Silhouette Special Edition

Romancing the Nanny #1818
Claiming the Rancher's Heart #1962

CINDY KIRK

is a lifelong Nebraska resident who started writing after taking a class at a local community college. But her interest in the written word started years before, when she was in her teens. At sixteen she wrote in her diary, "I don't know what I would do if I couldn't be a writer."

Not until her daughter was heading off to college did Cindy return to her first love—writing. Unlike some writers, Cindy wasn't interested in newspaper or magazine articles, short stories or poetry. When she decided to start writing, she jumped feetfirst into book-length fiction. She loves reading and writing romance as she believes in the power of love and in happily ever after. An incurable romantic, Cindy loves seeing her characters grow and learn from their mistakes and, in the process, achieve a happy ending.

She and her high school sweetheart husband live on an acreage with two cats...one of whom loves to sit next to the computer and supervise her writing. Cindy loves to hear from readers. She invites you to visit her Web site at www.CindyKirk.com.

This book is dedicated with a thankful heart to my fabulous critique partners Louise Foster, Renee Halverson and Ruth Kaufman.

Chapter One

"There's a whole herd of 'em." Stacie Summers stopped in the middle of the sidewalk and stared. Since arriving in Sweet River, Montana, two weeks ago she'd seen an occasional cowboy. But never so many. And never clustered together. "What's the occasion?"

Anna Anderssen, Stacie's friend and Sweet River native, came to a halt beside her. "What day is it?"

"Wednesday," Stacie answered.

"June second," Lauren Van Meveren replied. The doctoral student had seemed lost in thought since the three roommates had left Sharon's Food Mart. But now, standing beside Stacie in the bright sunlight, she couldn't have been more focused.

Though Lauren would normally be the first to

say that staring was rude, she watched the cowboys pile out of the Coffee Pot Café with undisguised interest.

"Wednesday, June second," Anna repeated. Her blue eyes narrowed in thought as she pulled a key fob from her pocket and unlocked the Jeep parked at the curb.

Stacie shifted the heavy sack of groceries to her other arm, opened the back and dropped the bag inside.

"Bingo," Anna announced with a decisive nod.

"They were playing bingo?" It seemed odd to Stacie that a group of men would gather on a Wednesday morning to play a game. But she'd quickly discovered that Sweet River was its own world.

"No, silly." Anna giggled. "The Cattleman's Association meets the first Wednesday of the month."

While that made more sense than bingo, Stacie wondered what issues such an organization would address. Ann Arbor, Michigan, where she'd grown up, was hardly a cattleman's paradise. And in the ten years she'd resided in Denver, not a single cowboy had crossed her path.

When Lauren had proposed moving to Anna's hometown to research male-female compatibility for her dissertation, Stacie had tagged along. The search for her perfect job—her bliss, as she liked to call it—wasn't going well, and a change of scenery seemed a good idea.

For some reason, she'd thought Sweet River would be like Aspen, one of her favorite towns. She'd expected cute, trendy shops and a plethora of doctors, lawyers and businessmen who enjoyed the great outdoors.

Boy, had she been wrong.

"I've never seen so many guys in boots and hats."

They were big men with broad shoulders, weathered skin and hair that had never seen a stylist's touch. Confident men who worked hard and lived life on their own terms. Men who would expect a wife to give up her dreams for a life on a ranch.

Though the air outside was warm, Stacie shivered.

Lauren's eyes took on a distant, almost dreamy look. "Do you know the first cowboys came from Mexico? They were known as *vaqueros,* the Spanish word for cowboys."

Stacie shot a pleading look in Anna's direction. They needed to stop Lauren before she got rolling. If not, they'd be forced to endure a lecture on the history of the modern cowboy all the way home.

"Get in, Lauren." Anna gestured to the Jeep. "We don't want the Rocky Road to melt."

Though Anna had injected a nice bit of urgency in her voice, Lauren's gaze remained riveted on the men, dressed in jeans and T-shirts and boots, talking and laughing in deep, manly voices.

One guy captured Stacie's attention. With his jeans, cowboy hat and sun-bronzed skin, he looked like all the others. Yet her gaze had been immediately drawn to him. It must have been because he was talking to Anna's brother, Seth. There could be no other explanation. A testosterone-rich male had never made it onto her radar before. She liked her men more artsy, preferring the starving-poet look over a bulky linebacker any day.

"You know, Stace—" Lauren tapped a finger against her lips "—something tells me there just may be a cowboy in your future."

Lauren's research involved identifying compatible couples, and Stacie was Lauren's first guinea pig—or as she liked to refer to it, research subject.

A knot formed in the pit of Stacie's stomach at the thought of being paired with a ropin', ridin' manly man. She sent a quick prayer heavenward. *Dear God, please. Anyone but a cowboy.*

A few weeks later, Stacie dropped into the high-backed wicker chair on Anna's porch, braced for battle. When Lauren had arrived home after an afternoon run, Stacie had told her they needed to talk. She'd stewed in silence about the prospect of Lauren's proposed match for her long enough.

While she knew it was important for Lauren's research that she at least meet this guy, it seemed wrong to waste his time. And hers.

Stacie was still formulating the "I'm not interested in a cowboy" speech for Lauren when a cool breeze from the Crazy Mountains ruffled the picture in her hand. She lifted her face, reveling in the feel of mountain air against her cheek. Even after four weeks in Big Sky country, Stacie still found herself awed by the beauty that surrounded her.

She glanced out over the large front yard. Everywhere she looked the land was lush and green. And the flowers…June had barely started and the bluebells, beargrass and Indian paintbrush were already in riotous bloom.

The screen door clattered shut, and Lauren crossed the porch, claiming the chair opposite Stacie. "What's up?"

Stacie pulled her gaze from the breathtaking scenery to focus on Lauren.

"Your computer hiccupped. It's the only explanation." Stacie lifted the picture. "Does he look like my type?"

"If you're talking about Josh Collins, he's a nice guy." Anna stepped onto the wraparound porch of the large two-story house and let the door fall shut behind her. "I've known him since grade school. He and my brother, Seth, are best friends."

Stacie stared in dismay at the teetering tray of drinks Anna was attempting to balance. Lauren, who was closest, jumped up and took the tray with the pitcher of lemonade and three crystal glasses from the perky blonde. "You're going to fall and break your neck wearing those shoes."

"Ask me if I care." Anna's gaze dropped to the lime-green, pointy-toed stilettos. "These are so me."

"They are cute," Lauren conceded. Her head cocked to one side. "I wonder if they'd fit me. You and I wear the same size—"

"Hel-lo." Stacie lifted a hand and waved it wildly. "Remember me? The one facing a date with Mr. Wrong? Any minute?"

"Calm down." Lauren poured a glass of lemon-ade, handed it to Stacie and sat down with a grace-fulness Stacie envied. "I don't make mistakes. If you recall, I gave you a summary of the results. Unless you lied on your survey or he lied on his, you and Josh Collins are very much compatible."

She wanted to believe her friend. After all, her first match with Sweet River attorney Alexander Darst had been pleasant. Unfortunately there'd been no spark.

Stacie lifted the picture of the rugged rancher and studied it again. Even if he hadn't been on a horse, even if she hadn't seen him talking with Seth after the Cattleman's Association meeting, his hat and boots confirmed her theory about a computer mal-function.

A match between a city girl and a rancher made no sense. Everyone knew city and country were like oil and water. They just didn't mix.

Sadly, for all her jokes about the process, she was disappointed. She'd hoped to find a summer com-panion, a Renaissance man who shared her love of cooking and the arts.

"He's a cowboy, Lauren." Stacie's voice rose despite her efforts to control it. *"A cowboy."*

"You got something against cowboys?"

The deep sexy voice coming from the front steps sent a jolt through Stacie. She dropped the picture to the table, turned in her seat and met an unblink-ing blue-eyed gaze.

It was *him*.

She had to admit he looked even better up close. He wore a chambray shirt that made his eyes look strikingly blue and a pair of jeans that hugged his long legs. There was no hat, just lots of thick, dark hair brushing his collar.

He continued to lazily appraise her. The glint in his eye told her he knew she'd put herself in a hole and was desperately searching for a way to shovel out.

Trouble was, she couldn't count on Lauren, who appeared to be fighting a laugh. Anna—well, Anna just stared expectantly at her, offering no assistance at all.

"Of course I like cowboys," Stacie said, feeling an urgent need to fill the silence that seemed to go on for hours but lasted only a few seconds. "Cowboys make the world go round."

His smile widened to a grin, and Lauren laughed aloud. Stacie shot her a censuring look. Granted, her response might not have been the best, but it could have been worse. She'd been caught off guard. Startled. Distracted. By his eyes...and his timing.

Why, oh, why, hadn't she kept her mouth shut?

"Well, I can't say I recall ever hearing that saying before," he said smoothly, "but it's definitely true."

Okay, so he was also gracious, a quality sadly lacking in most men she'd dated, and one she greatly admired. It was too bad he was not only a cowboy, but also so big. He had to be at least six-foot-two, with broad shoulders and a muscular build. Rugged. Manly. A dreamboat to many, but not *her* type at all.

Still, when those laughing blue eyes once again

settled on her, she shivered. There was keen intelligence in their liquid depths, and he exuded a self-confidence that she found appealing. This cowboy was nobody's fool.

Stacie opened her mouth to ask if he wanted a beer—he didn't look like a lemonade guy—but Anna spoke first.

"It's good to see you." Anna crossed the porch, her heels clacking loudly. When she reached Josh, she wrapped her arms around him. "Thank you for filling out the survey."

Josh smiled and gave her hair a tug. "Anything for you, Anna Banana."

Stacie exchanged a glance with Lauren.

"Anna Banana?" Lauren's lips twitched. "You never told us you had a nickname."

"Seth gave it to me when I was small," Anna explained before shifting her attention back to Josh. She wagged a finger at him. "You were supposed to forget that name."

"I have a good memory."

Stacie could see the twinkle in his eyes.

"I have a good memory, as well," Anna teased. "I remember Seth telling me that you and he preferred the traditional dating route. Yet, you both filled out Lauren's survey. Why?"

There was a warm, comfortable feel to the interaction between the two. Stacie found herself wondering if Josh and Anna had ever dated. A stab of something she couldn't quite identify rose up at the thought. It was almost as if she were…jealous? But that would be crazy. She wasn't interested in Josh Collins, cowboy extraordinaire.

"Seth probably did it because he knew you'd kill him if he didn't," Josh explained. "I completed the survey because Seth asked and I owed him a favor." He shoved his hands into his pockets and rocked back on his heels. "I never expected to get matched."

He's no more excited about this date than I am, Stacie thought, pushing back her chair and rising, finding the thought more comforting than disturbing.

"I'll try to make the evening as painless as possible." Stacie covered the short distance separating them and held out her hand. "I'm Stacie Summers, your date."

"I figured as much." He pulled a hand from his pocket and his fingers covered hers in a warm, firm grip. "Josh Collins."

To Stacie's surprise, a tingle traveled up her arm. She slipped her hand from his, puzzled by the reaction. The cute attorney's hand had brushed against hers several times during their date, and she hadn't felt a single sizzle.

"Would you care to join us?" Anna asked. "We have fresh-squeezed lemonade. And I could bring out the sugar cookies Stacie made this morning."

His easy smile didn't waver, but something told Stacie he'd rather break a bronc than drink lemonade and eat cookies with three women.

Though several minutes earlier she'd been determined to do whatever it took to cut this date short, she found herself coming to his rescue. "Sorry, Anna. Josh agreed to a date with one woman, not three."

Lauren rose and stepped forward. "Well, before my roommate steals you away, let me introduce myself. I'm Lauren Van Meveren, the author of the survey you took. I also want to extend my thanks to you for participating."

"Pleased to meet you, Lauren." Josh shook her hand. "Those were some mighty interesting questions."

Stacie exchanged a glance with Anna. Obviously Josh didn't realize he was in danger of opening the floodgates. If there was one thing Lauren was passionate about, it was her research.

"I'm working on my doctoral dissertation." Lauren's face lit up, the way it always did when anyone expressed interest in her research. "The survey is a tool to gather data that will either support or disprove my research hypothesis."

"Seth mentioned you were working on your Ph.D.," Josh said. "But when I asked what your research question was, he couldn't tell me."

Stacie stifled a groan. The floodgates were now officially open.

Lauren straightened. "You're familiar with the dissertation process?"

"Somewhat," he admitted. "My mother is working on her Ph.D. in nursing. I remember what she went through to get her topic approved."

"Then you do understand." Lauren gestured to the wicker chair next to hers. "Have a seat. I'll tell you about my hypothesis."

"I suggest we all sit down," Anna said with a

smile. "This may take a while," she added in a low tone only loud enough for Stacie to hear.

Stacie slipped back into the chair she'd vacated moments before. Josh snagged the seat beside her, his attention focused on Lauren. Even if Stacie wanted to save him, it was too late now.

Lauren's lips tipped up in a satisfied smile. "I was ecstatic when my subject was approved."

"And what are you studying?" Josh prompted.

Shoot me now, Stacie thought to herself. *Just put a gun to my head and shoot me.*

"Having relevant, personally tailored information about values and characteristics central to interpersonal relationships increases the chance of successful establishment and maintenance of said relationships," Lauren said without taking a breath. "It's a concept already embraced by many of the online dating services. But my study focuses more on what goes into forming a friendship rather than just a love match."

"Very interesting," Josh said, sounding surprisingly sincere. "What made you decide to do the research here?"

"Anna suggested I consider it—"

"I told her about all the single men." Anna poured a glass of lemonade and handed it to Josh. "And that I had a house where she could stay rent free. I decided to come along since there was nothing keeping me in Denver."

Josh shifted his attention to Anna. "Seth mentioned you lost your job."

"My employer was supposed to sell me her boutique." Anna took the last seat at the table. "Instead, she sold it to someone else."

Josh shook his head, sympathy in his eyes. "That sucks."

"Tell me about it," Anna said with a sigh.

The handsome cowboy seemed to be getting along so well with her roommates that Stacie wondered if anyone would notice if she got up and left. When her gaze returned to the table, she found Josh staring.

"It's been great catching up." He drained his glass of lemonade. "But Stacie and I should get going."

He stood, and Stacie automatically rose to her feet. She adored her roommates, but going with her match seemed a better option than staying and talking research with Lauren or rehashing job disappointments with Anna.

Josh followed her to the steps. Though he'd already given her a quick once-over when he'd first arrived, she caught him casting surreptitious glances her way.

If the look in his eye was any indication, her khaki capris and pink cotton shirt met with his approval. Stacie felt the tension in her shoulders begin to ease. Anna had said he was a nice guy, and his interactions with her roommates had shown that to be true.

There was certainly no need to be stressed. But when she started chattering about the weather, Stacie realized her nerves were on high alert.

But if Josh found the topic dull, he didn't show it. In fact, he seemed more than willing to talk about the lack of rain the area had been experiencing. He'd just started telling her about a particularly bad forest fire near Big Timber a couple years earlier, when they reached his black 4x4.

He reached around her to open the door. When she stepped forward, he offered her a hand up into the vehicle.

"Thank you, Josh."

"My pleasure." He coupled the words with an easy smile.

Her heart skipped a beat. She didn't know why she was so charmed. Maybe it was because Mr. Sweet River attorney had gotten an F in the manners department. He hadn't opened a single door for her or even asked what movie she wanted to see. Instead they'd watched an action flick *he'd* chosen.

Josh, on the other hand, not only opened the door without being asked, but he waited until she was settled inside the truck before shutting the door and rounding the front of the vehicle.

She watched him through the window, admiring his sure, purposeful stride. The cowboy exhibited a confidence that many women would find appealing. But as he slid into the driver's seat, her attention was drawn to the rifle hanging in the window behind her head. Her earlier reservations flooded back.

But how would she tell this nice guy that he wasn't her type?

"I can't get used to how flat the streets are," she said, buying herself some time. "When Anna talked about her hometown, I pictured a town high in the mountains, not one in a valley."

"It can be disappointing when things aren't what we expect," he said in an even tone.

"Not always." Stacie's gaze met his. "The unexpected can often be a pleasant surprise."

They drove in silence for several seconds.

"Did you know I'm psychic?"

She shifted in the seat to face him. "You are?"

"My powers," he continued, "are sending me a strong message."

"What's the message?" Stacie didn't know much about paranormal stuff, but she was curious. "What are your powers telling you?"

"You really want to know?" Josh's blue eyes looked almost black in the shadows of the truck's cab.

"Absolutely," Stacie said.

He stared unblinking. "They're telling me you don't want to be doing this."

Stacie stilled, and for a moment she forgot how to breathe. She adjusted her seat belt, not wanting to be rude and agree, but hating to lie. "What makes you say that?"

"For starters, what you said about cowboys." His smile took any censure from the words. "That, coupled with the look in your eye when you first saw me."

Though he gave no indication she'd hurt his feelings, she knew she had, and her heart twisted at the realization. "You seem very nice," she said softly. "It's just that I've always been attracted to a different kind of man."

His dark brows pulled together, and she could

see the puzzlement in his eyes. "There's more than one kind?"

"You know," she stumbled over her words as she tried to explain. "Guys who like to shop and go to the theater. A metrosexual kind of guy."

"You like feminine men?"

She laughed at the shock he tried so hard to hide. "Not feminine…just more sensitive."

"And cowboys aren't sensitive?"

"No, they aren't," Stacie said immediately, then paused. "Are they?"

"Not really." Josh lifted a shoulder. "Not the ones I know, anyway."

"That's what I thought," Stacie said with a sigh, wondering why she felt disappointed when the answer was just what she'd expected.

"So what you're saying is this match stands no chance of success," Josh said.

Stacie hesitated. To be fair, she should give him a shot. But wouldn't that only postpone the inevitable? Still, there was something about this cowboy…

Cowboy. The word hit her like a splash of cold water.

"No chance," Stacie said firmly.

Josh's gaze searched her face, and she could feel her cheeks heat beneath the probing glance.

"I appreciate the honesty," he said at last, his face showing no emotion. "For a second I thought you might disagree. Crazy, huh?"

For a second she *had* been tempted to argue…

until she'd come to her senses. Josh might be gentlemanly and have the bluest eyes she'd ever seen, but she could tell that they were too different.

"That doesn't mean we can't be friends," Stacie said. "Of course, you probably have plenty of friends."

"None as pretty as you," he said. He cleared his throat and slowed the truck to a crawl as they entered the business district. "If you're hungry we can grab a bite. Or I can show you the sites and give you some Sweet River history."

Stacie pondered the options. She wasn't in the mood to return to the house or to eat. Though Anna had given both her and Lauren a tour when they'd first moved to Sweet River, she didn't remember much of the town's history.

"Or I can take you home," he added.

"Not home." She immediately dismissed that option. Since they'd cleared the air, there was no reason they couldn't enjoy the evening. "How about you do the tour-guide thing? Then, if we feel like it, we can eat."

"Tour guide it is."

They cruised slowly through the small business district with the windows down. She learned that the corner restaurant had once been a bank and that the food mart had been resurrected by a woman who'd moved back to Sweet River after her husband died. He gave an interesting and informative travelogue, interspersed with touches of humor and stories from the past.

"…and then Pastor Barbee told Anna he didn't

care if she dressed it like a baby—she couldn't bring a lamb to church."

Laughter bubbled up inside Stacie and spilled from her lips.

"I can't believe Anna had a lamb for a pet." She couldn't keep a touch of envy from her voice. "My parents wouldn't even let me have a dog."

He looked at her in surprise. "You like dogs?"

"Love 'em."

"Me, too." He chuckled. "I better…I've got seven."

Stacie raised a brow. "Seven?"

"Yep."

She marveled that he could look so serious when telling such a tall tale.

"Wow, we have so much in common." Stacie deliberately widened her eyes. "You have seven dogs. I have seven pink ostriches."

Josh cast her a startled glance. "I'm serious."

"Yeah, right."

"Okay, one dog and six pups," he clarified. "Bert, my blue heeler, had puppies eight weeks ago."

He seemed sincere, but something still wasn't making sense. "Did you say *Bert* had puppies?"

"Her given name is Birdie." The look on his face told her what he thought of *that* name. "My mother chose it because Bert loves to chase anything with wings."

Stacie laughed. "I bet they're cute. The puppies, I mean."

"Want to see them?"

She straightened in her seat. "Could I?"

"If you don't mind a road trip," he said in a casual tone. "My ranch is forty miles from here."

He was letting her know that if she agreed, they'd be spending the rest of the day together. And he was giving her an out. But Stacie didn't hesitate. She adored puppies. And she was enjoying this time with Josh.

"It's a beautiful day," Stacie said, not even glancing at the sky. "Perfect for a drive."

"Don't give me that," he said, a smile returning to his face. "I've got your number. You don't care about the drive. Or the weather. This is all about the dogs."

"Nuh-uh." Stacie tried to keep a straight face but couldn't keep from laughing.

He did have her number. And she hoped this *was* all about the dogs. Because if it wasn't, she was in big trouble.

Chapter Two

Josh pulled up in front of his weathered ranch house and wondered when he'd lost his mind. Was it when he'd first seen the dark-haired beauty sitting on the porch and felt that stirring of attraction? Or when he'd started talking about the weather and she'd listened with rapt attention? Or maybe when her eyes had lit up like Christmas tree lights when he'd mentioned the puppies?

Whatever the reason, bringing her to the ranch had been a mistake.

He cast a sideways glance and found her staring wide-eyed, taking it all in. When her gaze lingered on the peeling paint, he fought the urge to explain that he had brushes and rollers and cans of exterior latex in the barn ready to go once he got the rest of the cattle moved. But he kept his mouth shut.

It didn't matter what she thought of his home; it was his and he was proud of it. Situated on the edge of the Gallatin National Forest and nestled at the base of the Crazy Mountains, the land had been in his family for five generations. When he'd first brought Kristin here as a bride the house had been newly painted and remodeled. Still, she'd found fault.

"It's so—" Stacie began, then stopped.

Shabby. Old. Isolated. His mind automatically filled in the words his wife—ex-wife, he corrected himself—had hurled at him whenever they'd argued.

"Awesome." Stacie gazed over the meadow east of the house, already blue with forget-me-nots. "Like your own little piece of paradise."

Surprised, Josh exhaled the breath he didn't realize he'd been holding.

"Oh-h." Stacie squealed and leaned forward, resting her hands on the dash, her gaze focused on the short-haired dog, with hair so black it almost looked blue, streaking toward the truck. "Is that Bert?"

Josh smiled and pulled to a stop in front of the house. "That's her."

"I can't wait to pet her."

Out of the corner of his eye, Josh saw her reach for the door handle. Before she could push it open, he grabbed her arm. "Let me get the door."

"That's okay." Stacie tugged at his firm grasp. "I'll let you off being gentlemanly this once."

"No." Josh tightened his fingers around her arm. When her gaze dropped to the hand encircling her arm, he released his grip, knowing he had some quick explaining to do. "Bert can be territorial. You're a stranger. I'm not sure how she'll react to you."

He didn't want to scare Stacie, but last week the UPS man had stopped by and Bert had bared her teeth.

"Oh." A startled look crossed Stacie's face and she sank back in the seat. "Of course. I don't know why that never occurred to me."

"She'll probably be fine," he said a trifle gruffly, disturbed by the protective feelings rising in him. "I just don't want to take any chances."

A look of gratitude filled her eyes but he pretended not to notice. He pushed open the door and stepped from the truck. He didn't need her thanks. He'd do this for any woman, including old Miss Parsons, who'd rapped his knuckles with a ruler in third grade. Yep, he'd do this for any female, not just for a pretty one that made him feel like a schoolboy again.

Josh shifted his attention to the predominantly black-and-gray-colored dog that stood at his feet, her white-tipped tail wagging wildly.

"Good girl." He reached down and scratched Bert's head. She'd been a birthday gift from his mother, six months before Kristin moved out. She'd never liked the dog. But then, by the time she left, Kristin hadn't liked much of anything; not the ranch, the house or him.

"Can I get out now?"

Josh grinned at the impatient voice coming from the truck's cab. Shoving aside thoughts of the past, he hurried to her door, Bert at his heels.

He paused and dropped his gaze to the dog. "Sit."

Bert did as instructed, her intelligent, amber-colored eyes riveted to him, ears up, on full alert.

"Miss Summers is a friend, Bert," Josh warned as he opened the passenger door. "Be good."

Despite the warning, the hair on Bert's neck and back rose as the brunette exited the vehicle. Josh moved between her and the dog.

"Nice doggie." Stacie's voice was low and calm as she slipped around him. She took a step forward and held out her hand. "Hello, Bert. I'm Stacie."

Casting a look at Josh, Bert took a couple steps forward and cautiously sniffed Stacie's outstretched hand. Then, to Josh's surprise, Bert began to lick her fingers.

"Thank you, Birdie. I like you, too." Stacie's smile widened as the dog continued to lick her. "I can't wait to see your babies. I bet they're pretty, like their mama."

Bert's tail swished from side to side and Josh stared in amazement. For a woman who'd grown up without pets, Stacie certainly had a way with animals.

"Australian cattle dogs—that's another name for blue heelers—are known for being smart and loyal. They're great with livestock." Josh paused. "Still, not many would call them pretty—"

"She's *very* pretty." Stacie bent over and clasped

her hands over the dog's ears, shooting Josh a warning look.

"My apologies." Josh covered his smile with a hand. "Would you like to see the six smaller versions in the barn?"

"Are you crazy?" Stacie straightened and grabbed his hand. "Let's go."

Her hand felt small in his, but there was firmness in the grasp that bespoke an inner strength. When he'd discovered that he'd been matched with Anna's friend from Denver, he'd wondered if Anna had monkeyed with the results.

He realized now that he and Stacie had more in common than he'd first thought. And he found himself liking this city girl. Of course that didn't mean she was a good match.

He'd been with a city girl once. Fell in love with her. Married her. But he was smarter now. This time he'd keep his heart to himself.

"I feel guilty." Josh stabbed the last piece of apple dumpling with his fork. "You spent the whole evening in the kitchen."

Stacie took a sip of coffee and smiled at the exaggeration. She hadn't spent the *entire* evening in the kitchen. They'd played with the puppies for the longest time. After that Josh had shown her all Bert's tricks, including catching a Frisbee in midair. By then, they were both hungry and she'd offered to make dinner.

"I told you," Stacie said, relishing the taste of the rich Columbian brew against her tongue. "Cooking is a hobby of mine. I love making something out of nothing."

Josh lowered his fork to rest on his now-empty plate. "You've impressed me. That noodle thing with the sausage and peppers tasted like something I'd get in a restaurant."

"And we didn't even have to go out." Stacie glanced around the modern country kitchen. After seeing the outside of the house, she'd been a bit apprehensive about the inside. But when Josh had ushered her through the front door and given her a tour, she'd been pleasantly surprised.

While the exterior needed some attention, the interior was up-to-date and exceptionally clean. When she'd complimented Josh on his tidiness, he sheepishly admitted that he had a housekeeper who came during the week to cook and clean.

"I'd have taken you out," Josh said, his gaze meeting hers. "I hope you know that."

"I do," Stacie said. "But this was more fun."

"I agree." Josh smiled and the fine lines that fanned out from the corners of his eyes crinkled appealingly. He pushed back his chair. "How 'bout we take our coffee into the family room?"

Stacie rose. Her gaze lingered on the dishes in the sink before returning to the ones still on the table.

"Don't even think about it." He placed his hand in the small of her back and nudged her toward the doorway. "I'll clean up later."

Moments later, Stacie was sitting on a burgundy leather sofa listening to Josh finish his story about the fire that had threatened 180,000 acres several years earlier.

"I was fortunate," Josh said. "The damage to my property was minimal. It could have been so much worse."

Stacie studied the rugged cowboy who sat on the sofa a mere foot away from her. "You love it, don't you?"

He tilted his head. "Love what?"

"The land. Your life here," Stacie said. "I see it in your eyes. Hear it in your voice. This is your passion."

"From the time I was small, all I've wanted to do was be a rancher." His expression turned serious. "This land is part of me, and it will be part of my legacy."

"What about your parents?" Stacie asked, realizing that up to this point they hadn't discussed family at all. "Are they around?"

"They live in Sweet River," Josh said. "My dad runs the bank. My mother is the director of nursing at the hospital."

Bank? Hospital? "I thought you'd grown up on a ranch?"

"I did," he said in a matter-of-fact tone. "But my father was never into it. As soon as I returned home from college, he turned the place over to me."

"Sounds like the passion for the land skipped a generation," Stacie said in a light tone.

Josh lifted a shoulder in a shrug. "It's a great life, but definitely not for everyone."

Stacie wished *her* family had the same attitude. Why couldn't they understand that what worked for them didn't work for her? That's why she'd gone away to college and stayed in Denver after graduation rather than returning to Michigan. She wanted to find *her* passion, *her* purpose, not lead a life she hadn't chosen.

A coyote howled in the distance, the eerie sound drifting in on the breeze through the screened patio door. Stacie shivered. "It's so quiet out here…so isolated. Do you ever get lonely?"

"I have friends." The smile that had hovered on the edge of his lips most of the evening disappeared and his shoulders stiffened. "I see my parents at least weekly."

"But you live by yourself." Stacie wasn't sure why she was pressing the issue, but the answer somehow seemed important. "Almost an hour from civilization."

"Sometimes I get lonely," he said. "But when I have a family of my own, it'll be different."

"The solitude would drive me bonkers." Stacie took a sip of coffee. "I need people. The more the merrier."

"It's important to know what you want and what you don't." Josh's expression gave nothing away. "I need to find a woman who could be happy with this kind of life."

"Cross me off that list," Stacie said, keeping her tone light.

Josh's gaze never left her face. "I've never been much for lists."

Regardless of his obvious reluctance to hurt her feelings, she knew he'd made his decision, just like she'd made hers. No matter what the computer thought, she and Josh weren't meant to ride together into the sunset.

She took another sip of coffee and gazed out the screen door, feeling a little sad at the thought. Which made absolutely no sense at all. "The good thing is we haven't completed our first date and we already know it's not going to work."

"What's so good about that?"

Didn't he understand that she was doing her best to see the glass as half-full? "We don't have to waste time—"

"Are you saying tonight was a waste?"

She exhaled an exasperated breath. "No, but—"

"I don't think it was a waste at all," he said. "I can't remember the last time I've had this much fun or ate such a delicious meal."

He smiled and her pulse skipped a beat. Yikes. She'd never thought a cowboy could be so sexy.

Stacie placed her cup on the coffee table. "I should be getting home."

"Not yet." Josh reached forward and gently touched her face, letting his finger glide along her jaw.

He's going to kiss me. He's going to kiss me. He's going to kiss me.

The words ran through her head like a mantra. She told herself to pull away. To put some distance between them. To just say no. He was Anna's friend, after all, and he was looking for someone special. But instead of moving back, she leaned into his caress, her body quivering with anticipation.

He moved closer. Then closer still. So close she could see the flecks of gold in his eyes and feel his breath upon her cheek. She was already anticipating the taste of his lips when he abruptly sat back, his hand dropping to his side. "This is a bad idea."

Her heart dropped like a lead balloon and she felt like a child whose favorite toy had been snatched from her grasp.

For several heartbeats they simply looked at each other.

"You're right." Her pulse, which had stalled, began to thump like a bass drum. "It's late. I should get home."

When she stood he didn't try to stop her. By the time she reached the front door, her heart had settled into a regular rhythm. She paused on the porch and took a deep breath of crisp mountain air, hoping it would clear her tangled thoughts. Darkness had fallen, but thanks to a brilliant moon and a sky filled with stars, she could see clearly.

Out of the corner of her eye, she saw Bert racing across the yard toward her. Her spirits lifted and she stopped at the base of the porch steps to give the dog a goodbye hug. Bert reciprocated with a wet kiss to her cheek. She laughed and gave the animal another quick squeeze.

When she straightened, she found Josh staring.

"What can I say?" she said. "Animals love me."

"Of course they do," she thought she heard him mutter under his breath.

Though the truck in the drive was less than twenty

feet away, the walk seemed to take forever. She quickly discovered that heeled sandals and a gravel drive weren't a good combination. Not to mention that every time she took a step, Bert pushed against her, forcing her closer to Josh.

When they got to the pickup, Josh reached past her to open the passenger door. Stacie inhaled the spicy scent of his aftershave and a yearning to play "kiss the cowboy" returned.

But instead of giving into temptation, she stepped back, putting a more comfortable distance between them. She was congratulating herself on her good sense when sharp teeth sank into the back of her heel. She yelped and leapt forward, crashing against Josh's broad chest.

His arms closed protectively around her and a look of concern blanketed his face. "What's wrong?"

Stacie turned in his embrace to cast the dog a reproachful look. "Birdie bit the back of my foot."

The animal cocked her head and swished her tail slowly. Her dark lips curved upward until it almost looked as if she were smiling.

"Nipping heels is one of the ways she herds cattle," Josh said in an apologetic tone. "It's her nature."

"I don't like that part of her nature." Stacie wagged a finger at Bert. "Don't do that again."

The dog stared for a moment and then lifted a paw and proceeded to lick it.

"She's sorry," Josh said, a little smile tugging at the corners of his lips.

"Yeah, right." If Stacie didn't know better she'd

believe the animal had wanted her in Josh's arms and had done what she could to make that happen.

"Nothing will ever hurt you," Josh said, his eyes dark and intense. "Not on my watch."

"Are you saying the cowboy will protect me against the big, bad dog?" she asked in a teasing tone.

"Most definitely." His gaze drifted to her lips.

Though she knew she was playing with fire, Stacie slipped her arms around his neck, raking her fingers through his thick, wavy hair. "What I want to know is, who's going to protect me against *you?*"

She wasn't sure he heard the question. Because the words had barely left her lips when his mouth closed over hers.

Chapter Three

"You kissed her?" Seth Anderssen let out a hoot of laughter that echoed throughout the Coffee Pot Café.

Josh scowled and wrapped his fingers around the small cup, wishing he'd kept his big mouth shut. After all, Seth's sister, Anna, was Stacie's friend. If Seth mentioned to her he'd been blabbing about the date, it might get back to Stacie. And she might get the mistaken impression that he was interested. Which he wasn't. Not in the least.

"Did she come back into the house?" Seth asked in an all-too-innocent tone. "So you two could get even better acquainted?"

Josh met his friend's blue eyes. "Are you asking if I slept with her?"

Though no one was seated nearby, Josh had automatically lowered his voice. When his marriage crumbled he'd provided more than his share of grist for the town's gossip mill, and he wasn't eager to repeat the experience.

Seth's gaze remained steady. "Did you?"

"Of course not." Josh responded immediately, making sure his tone left no room for doubt. "We just met. Besides, she's not my type. And I am *not* hers, either. She told me so."

A smile quirked the corners of Seth's lips. "Tell that to someone who'll believe it."

"She's Anna's friend." Josh ground out the words, irritated at the teasing, yet not sure why. Seth had always liked to rattle his cage. Why should now be any different?

"She's also very pretty," Seth pointed out.

"She's a city girl," Josh continued. "A hothouse flower not suited to this climate."

Just like Kristin, he thought.

"Sometimes those hybrid varieties can surprise you—"

"Then *you* go out with her—" Josh stopped himself, finding the thought of Stacie dating Seth strangely disturbing.

"I'm not her perfect match." Seth took a sip of coffee. "You are."

The words hung in the air for a long moment.

"I don't believe that bull," Josh said finally. "Look at Kristin and me. Everyone said we were a perfect match. Didn't even make it three years."

Though he now realized they were better off apart, the failure of his marriage still rankled. When he'd said his vows, he'd meant every word. He'd been willing to do whatever it took to make it work. But he'd learned the hard way that for a marriage to succeed, both parties had to share that commitment.

"That's because you and the wicked witch weren't matched by a computer."

"Get real. You don't believe in that stuff any more than I do."

"I filled out the questionnaires, didn't I?"

"Only 'cause you knew Anna would have your hide if you didn't."

"Speaking of which…" Seth's gaze settled on the doorway. "We got us some company."

Even before Josh turned around he knew who he'd find standing there. The click-clack of heels had been his first clue. The light scent of jasmine mingling with the smell of café cooking grease was the giveaway.

"Stacie…Anna…what a surprise." Josh pushed back his chair to stand, but Anna waved him down.

"Stay put," Anna said. "We're not staying. I saw Seth's truck parked out front and had a quick question for him."

Seth leaned back in his chair and lifted the coffee cup to his lips. "What can I do for you, baby sister?"

"I need more men." Anna cast a sideways glance at Stacie. "I mean, *we* need more men."

"I'm sorry Josh wasn't man enough for you." Seth's gaze focused on Stacie and his tone oozed sympathy.

Josh shot him a dark glance, warning him to back off.

The merest hint of a twinkle in Seth's eyes was his only response.

"I never said that." Stacie's cheeks turned a becoming shade of pink as her eyes sought his.

"Seth is a joker," Josh said, offering her a reassuring smile. He hated seeing her distressed. Her worried frown brought out his protective instincts and he wanted nothing more than to take her in his arms...

Whoa...where had that come from? He reined in the emotion and told himself he was merely reacting to her appearance.

After all, she looked as pretty as the bluebells that filled his pasture. Instead of wearing jeans like most women in Sweet River, she had on a pair of shorts the color of the summer sky and a sleeveless, loose-fitting white shirt with something blue underneath.

Though the shorts came down midthigh and the shirt wasn't at all revealing, Josh remembered the feel of that body against his. In fact, he could still taste the sweetness of her lips and feel the softness of her hair against his cheek...

"I'm game," Seth's voice broke into his thoughts. "How 'bout you, Josh?"

Josh refocused to find the three staring expectantly at him. He quickly considered his options. He could admit that his mind had been traveling down a dead-end road or he could just go along. After all, Seth had already agreed. "Okay by me."

"Great." Anna smiled. "We'll see you at eight."

With their business concluded, the two women turned and headed for the door, admiring looks following in their wake.

"Should be interesting," Seth said.

"What?"

Seth grinned. "I knew you weren't listening."

It wasn't the smile that worried Josh; it was the gleam in Seth's eye. A sinking feeling filled the pit of Josh's stomach. "Tell me."

"Anna wants me to round up some more guys for the survey," Seth said. "Most ranchers from the area will be at the dance tonight. I promised I'd ask around."

A rush of relief flowed through Josh. For a second, he'd let his imagination soar. "So all we have to do is recruit?"

"That's all *I* have to do," Seth said. "You have a different assignment."

Josh stilled. Why did he have the uneasy feeling the other shoe was about to drop? "Which is?"

"You're escorting Stacie to the dance." Seth motioned to the waitress for more coffee. "When the guys see how good your match turned out, Anna figures they'll want one of their own."

"This doesn't feel right." Stacie stared in the mirror and frowned. Dressed in blue jeans and a long-sleeved shirt with pearl snaps, she looked more like an extra in a Hollywood Western than a stylish twenty-first-century woman.

"I knew it." Anna's gaze dropped to Stacie's feet,

to the Tony Lamas they'd picked up in town. "I thought you should have gone up a half size—"

"They fit fine." Stacie hastened to reassure her. If boots were indeed de rigueur for country dances, she'd found her fashion statement. The pink crunch goats had been the prettiest the Montana Western store had to offer.

"O-kay." Anna tilted her head, confusion clouding her blue eyes. "If it's not the boots, what doesn't fit?"

All the misgivings that had been plaguing Stacie since she first heard Anna's plan surged forth. "Me. Josh. This going-to-the-dance-together bit. I don't want to do it."

Anna's eyes widened as though this was the first she'd heard of Stacie's misgivings. Which didn't make sense, considering they'd been having this discussion off and on since Anna dropped the bombshell in the café. Frankly she'd been stunned when Josh agreed to the plan. When he'd taken her home after their first—and only—date, it had been clear to both of them that a romance wasn't going to work.

"I thought you liked him." Anna sounded hurt. As if Stacie was dissing her friend.

"I told you before…Josh is a wonderful guy." Stacie dropped on the bed and heaved a heavy sigh. "But he's not the man for me. And this—" she fingered the collar of her cowgirl shirt "—this isn't me."

For a moment Anna didn't say anything. Then she sashayed across the room, the rhinestones in her jean skirt glittering in the light. Once she reached the bed, she plopped down next to Stacie. "I'm not saying you have to stay in Sweet River and marry the guy. Just go to the dance with him. Have some fun."

"Going as his date just seems so…" Stacie struggled to find the words that would convey her feelings without insulting her friend.

Anna met her gaze. "Deceitful?"

Stacie nodded, relieved that Anna finally understood. "We *were* matched, but we aren't a couple."

"I believe," Anna pressed a finger to her lips, a contemplative look on her face, "you're thinking too hard."

Stacie blinked, stunned. It was the type of dismissive response she usually got from her family…as if she were too stupid to understand. She expected it from them, not from her roommate.

She lifted her chin, but when she met Anna's gaze, there was no condescension in the liquid blue depths.

"Why do you think most of the guys filled out the survey?" Anna asked when she remained silent.

"Because your brother made 'em."

"Good answer." Anna smiled. "Why else?"

"Because they're lonely and looking for their soul mates."

"Perhaps," Anna conceded. "Why else?"

Stacie shifted under Anna's expectant stare.

"Marriage or even a long-term relationship isn't really what Lauren's study is about," Anna explained.

"It's not?" Stacie couldn't keep the surprise from

her voice. Though Lauren's dissertation topic wasn't fixed in her mind, she'd been sure the bottom line was matchmaking.

"You and Josh have a lot in common, right?"

Stacie thought for a moment. "I like to cook. He likes to eat."

Anna's lips twitched. "What else?"

"We both love animals," Stacie added, warming to the topic. "And he's easy to talk to."

"You enjoyed his company," Anna said matter-of-factly. "He enjoyed yours."

Stacie nodded. She couldn't deny it. In fact, when Josh had driven her home that night, he'd taken the long way, giving them more time to talk. He hadn't been uncomfortable, despite what happened. And though he hadn't kissed her again, the look in his eyes had told her he wanted to…

"Some guys *are* looking for a wife." Anna stood and moved to the mirror, pulling her long blond hair up in a ponytail before letting it drop back down. "But a lot of them would be satisfied with simply meeting someone who enjoys their company. Someone to go out with and have a good time. Someone to be their friend and take the edge off their loneliness."

Stacie took a moment to digest Anna's words. She thought back to her evening with Josh. She'd had fun and knew he had, too. Maybe that *was* enough.

"Okay. I'll do it," Stacie said reluctantly, hoping she wasn't making a mistake. "I'll do it. But I refuse to wear a hat. And square dancing is absolutely out."

Chapter Four

"All jump up and never come down, swing your pretty girl round and round."

Stacie twirled, the pink boots sliding on the sawdust-covered dance floor. Her breath came in short puffs and her heart danced a happy rhythm in her chest.

The large wooden structure that housed the Sweet River Civic Center was filled to capacity. The dance floor, brought in specifically for the occasion, took up a good third of the building. The rest was filled with tables decorated with red-and-white-checkered table-cloths. Baskets of peanuts doubled as a centerpiece.

Food supplied by ladies in the community sat on tables against a far wall, next to kegs of beer.

Though many of the younger men and women had left the floor when the square-dance caller took the stage, Stacie and Josh had stayed. She adjusted Josh's cowboy hat more firmly on her head during the promenade, a smile lifting the corners of her lips.

She'd been determined to remain hat free. But when Josh teasingly plopped his Stetson on her head, declaring her the prettiest cowgirl he'd ever seen, it seemed right to leave it there. And when the square dance had started and he asked her to give it a try, she hadn't had the heart to say no.

Surprisingly Stacie found herself enjoying the experience. But she hadn't realized how exhausting this style of dancing could be. The two-step and country swing moves had been challenging, but this—she allemanded left for what seemed like forever—set her heart pounding and turned her breathing ragged.

When the set ended and the caller started up again Stacie shook her head at Josh's questioning look. They'd barely relinquished their spot when an older couple took their place. Though it was almost midnight, the party showed no sign of slowing down.

Stacie wove her way through the tables, hopping aside just in time to avoid being plowed over by a drunken cowboy with a ten-gallon hat.

Josh slipped an arm around her shoulders, sheltering her with his body. He shot the man a quelling glance. "Watch where you're going, Danker. You almost ran into the lady."

Danker—all 285 pounds of him—stopped and turned. Stacie had never liked bulky linebacker types. Their size made her uneasy. But not this guy. With his chocolate-brown eyes and thick curly hair, he wasn't a grizzly but a teddy bear.

A huge, *drunk* teddy bear. His glassy eyes fought to focus.

"I did what? Oh." His gaze shifted from Josh to Stacie and a big grin split his face. "Is this her? Your new honey?"

"This is Stacie Summers," Josh said, then proceeded to introduce her to Wes Danker.

She learned that Wes raised sheep and that his ranch was twenty miles from Josh's spread. But when Josh mentioned Wes had recently returned to Sweet River after a stint in a Wall Street brokerage firm, Stacie couldn't hide her surprise.

"I need another drink," the man bellowed, punctuating his words with a belch.

Josh's gaze narrowed. "Tell me you're staying in town tonight and sleeping this off."

Wes's expression brightened as his gaze returned to Stacie. "I could sleep with you. If'n you'd let me."

Josh's blue eyes turned to slivers of silver in the light. "Ain't gonna happen."

Wes let loose a hearty laugh. "I was just kiddin'. I know she's yours." His expression sobered. "I wish I had a woman."

"That's why you need to fill out the survey," a familiar voice responded. Seth pushed through the crowd to stand beside Wes. "I told you, buddy. You want a woman. You fill out a survey."

"Probably won't get matched anyway." Wes grabbed two full plastic cups out of the hands of a man passing by. He took a big gulp out of one and then the other.

The cowboy whose beers he'd stolen just laughed and continued through the crowd.

"You won't know if you don't try." Seth's gaze settled on Stacie and Josh. "Look at Collins. Who'd a thought he'd get matched?"

"Hey." Josh gave Seth a shove. "Watch it."

"I want one as pretty as her," Wes said, as if placing an order for a side of fries, his gaze lingering on Stacie.

Was it only her imagination or did Josh's arm tighten around her shoulders?

Seth slapped the big man on the back. "You stop over at Anna's house tomorrow, fill out that survey and she'll do her best."

"'Kay." Wes finished off the beer in his right hand and crushed the plastic cup between his massive fingers. "I gotta take a leak."

As he stumbled off, Stacie swallowed the laughter bubbling in her throat. "I cannot imagine him on Wall Street."

A smile lifted the corners of Josh's lips. "He was good at what he did. Made bucket loads of money."

"Sounds as if he's going to do the survey." Stacie slanted an admiring glance at Seth. "Anyone ever tell you that you are one fantastic recruiter?"

Seth winked. "I'm not done yet." His eyes settled

on a group of cowboys at a nearby table. "Five more and I make my quota."

Without a backward glance, he was gone.

"I hope Wes finds someone." Josh's expression turned thoughtful. "Though he's not at his best to-night, he's a good guy. Moving back to take over the ranch when his dad got sick was hard on him. I know he's lonely."

Stacie's heart went out to the gentle giant. In the past couple weeks she'd discovered what Anna had told her and Lauren was true: there simply weren't enough females to go around. Tonight, guys out-numbered women three to one.

"Seth is certainly doing his part to help make some matches," Stacie murmured as Josh led her to a table far from the dance floor. "Above and beyond the call of duty."

"He loves his sister." Josh pulled out a folding chair for Stacie. Once she sat down, he dropped into the chair next to her.

She thought Josh was clearly the handsomest man in the room. She inhaled deeply and her heart flut-tered. He smelled good, too. The spicy scent of his cologne set her pulse racing.

"He's happy to have her back in Sweet River," Josh added.

"My parents and siblings would be happy if I were back in Ann Arbor, too," Stacie said with a wry smile. "It's hard to run my life from a distance."

Josh pulled a basket that sat in the middle of the table closer and grabbed a couple of peanuts. He handed one to Stacie. "I don't think you mentioned your family at all the other evening."

"Be glad," Stacie intoned in a ghoulish whisper. "Be very, very glad."

Josh didn't laugh or change the subject as she expected. Instead, with his gaze firmly fixed on her, he cracked the shell in his hand. "I take it you don't get along."

"I wouldn't say that." Stacie fought to keep her tone light. She never wanted to be one of those people who whined about their life or their awful childhood. It could be so much worse. After all, high aspirations for your child could hardly be considered abuse. "They're all very successful. I'm the token low achiever."

Josh's gaze searched hers. "Believing your family doesn't respect and value the person you've become has to hurt."

"Their opinion doesn't bother me." A lump rose in her throat at his sympathetic tone, but she shoved it back down. "Most of the time, anyway."

Looking for an excuse to avoid his perceptive gaze, Stacie grabbed more peanuts. She shelled one and popped it into her mouth. By the time she met his gaze, her emotions were firmly under control. "Fact is, they're probably right."

His eyes never left hers. "You don't believe that."

Stacie hesitated, not wanting to lie, yet seeing no reason to bare her soul, either. "Sometimes I do. Other times, I tell myself it's just that I don't define success the same way they do."

"That's the way it was for me in college." Josh's eyes took on a faraway look. "Most of the guys I knew were all about making money. All I wanted to do was come back here and be a rancher."

"That's what I want, too." She paused and then laughed at the startled look on his face, realizing what she'd said. "No. No. I didn't—and don't— want to be a rancher. I simply want to be happy doing my life's work. But unlike you, I haven't found the avenue to my bliss."

Surprisingly, Josh didn't laugh. Instead, his expression grew even more serious. "If you could do anything, what would you do?"

He appeared sincerely interested and his tone invited confidences. Unfortunately over the years she'd learned the dangers of sharing her dreams. She'd discovered most men would happily run her life if she let them. Still, Josh didn't seem the kind to tell her what to do.

As if sensing her turmoil, Josh smiled encouragingly. "C'mon, tell me. I can keep a secret."

Maybe she'd gotten overheated on the dance floor and it had addled her brain. Maybe it was the knowledge that Josh was a man who understood money wasn't everything. Or maybe the beers she'd enjoyed this evening had loosened her tongue.

"I'd own a catering company and create fun dishes." She'd given up talking about her dream when it looked like it would never be a reality. "There's nothing I love more than parties and cooking and being creative. To be able to do that every day…it would be incredible."

A longing so intense it took her breath away rose up inside her. She thought she'd buried that dream, but intense emotion told her embers still smoldered.

"Based on the dinner you made the other night, I can see you being very successful." His supportive words and the sincerity in his tone warmed her heart. "Though I imagine you'd have to live in a large city to have enough clients to make a go of it."

"I did a business plan several years ago." Stacie flushed, embarrassed by the admission, yet not sure why. While she'd majored in business only because her father had insisted, she had to admit that some of what she'd learned occasionally came in handy. "The results surprised me."

Josh raised a brow. "What did you discover?"

"That it wouldn't have to be in New York or Los Angeles," Stacie said. "Or even in a city the size of Denver. A town with a population as little as two hundred thousand would work."

A look Stacie couldn't identify crossed Josh's face. It was gone quickly and his warm blue eyes refocused on her. "In this part of the world, you'd have to add the populations of Billings, Missoula and Great Falls together to get over two hundred thousand."

"Wow," Stacie said. "I guess I didn't realize those towns were so small. It—"

"Stacie, you've got to come with me." Lauren stood beside the table, looking very much the part of the local scene in her tight-fitting Wranglers and cowboy hat.

Lauren's mission tonight was to mingle and to be on the dance floor as much as possible. She'd encouraged Anna and Stacie to do the same, saying it would be good advertising.

But if Lauren had come to drag her back on the dance floor, it wasn't going to happen. Stacie's feet ached and she was enjoying her conversation with Josh too much to cut it short. "I'm kinda busy at the moment."

"I'm afraid it can't wait. Or rather, your brother won't wait." Lauren's gaze shifted from Stacie to Josh, then back to Stacie again. "He insists on speaking with you *now*."

Stacie dug her fingers into Josh's shirtsleeve. Paul called periodically, usually leaving a message about some job opportunity he thought she should pursue. But Saturday night was family time in his household. He'd never interrupt his time with his wife and children to call his sister. And why call Lauren and not her? Unless it was bad news and he knew she'd need her friend's support...

Dear God, had something happened to one of her parents? Her relationship with them might be tense at times, but she loved them dearly. She jumped to her feet. "Did he tell you what happened?"

She sensed rather than saw Josh move to stand beside her and then felt his arm slide around her waist, holding her steady.

"Paul isn't on the phone," Lauren explained. "He's here in Sweet River. Flew into Billings and drove straight over. He's waiting by the entrance for you."

The puzzle pieces that had begun to lock into place suddenly didn't fit. "Why would he come all this way to give me bad news?"

The confusion on Lauren's face was quickly replaced with understanding. "I'm not sure why he's here, but it's definitely not for that. I asked him how the family was, he said fine."

Stacie exhaled the breath she'd been holding and closed her eyes. Thank you, God.

"Why do you suppose he's here?" Josh asked.

"No idea." Stacie straightened her shoulders and shifted her gaze to Lauren. "Take me to him."

Josh stepped forward. "I'll come with you."

"No." The word came out more sharply than she'd intended. Stacie immediately softened the response with a smile. "Thank you, but no."

The last thing she wanted was to subject Josh to Paul's imperious manner or for her brother to get the wrong idea about her relationship with Josh.

"Are you sure?" Doubt filled his eyes and a frown worried his brow.

"Positive." Stacie removed his hat from her head and held it out to him. "Thanks for the loaner."

Josh took the hat, but didn't immediately put it on his head. "I don't understand why he'd show up here."

It was a question she'd like answered, as well. "No clue," Stacie said. "But I'm going to find out."

Chapter Five

Josh watched Stacie and Lauren disappear from sight, adrenaline spurting through his veins.

Though she hadn't said anything about Paul, the fact that she wasn't close to any of her family meant she wasn't close to this guy, either. And even though this wasn't a date in the traditional sense, Stacie had come with him. That meant he was responsible for her safety.

His mind made up, Josh pushed through the crowd, responding to friends without slowing his pace. He reached the front entrance, expecting to see Stacie and her brother, but instead found Pastor Barbee and his wife standing by the door.

The midsixties couple had been on the dance

floor since the square dancing started, so Josh hadn't had a chance to say hello much less introduce Stacie. He could only hope they knew who she was.

"Have you seen Stacie Summers?" Josh kept his tone casual and offhand. "She's Anna's friend. The one I was dancing with earlier."

"The pretty dark-haired girl." Mrs. Barbee nodded approvingly. "With the pink boots."

"That's the one." Josh cast a quick glance around, but once again came up empty. "You saw her?"

"She went outside." The pastor gestured toward the door with one hand.

"She was with a man," Mrs. Barbee added, a look of sympathy on her lined face. "Nice looking, but not as handsome as you."

Josh wasn't quite sure how to respond to that statement so he let it lie.

"Appreciate the information." Josh opened the door and stepped into the cool night air. He paused on the sidewalk and scanned the familiar street. At the far end of the block, he spotted her.

She and her brother stood next to a late-model Lincoln Town Car. Though her arms were crossed and her spine as stiff as a soldier's, she didn't appear in any distress. Now that he knew she was okay, good manners dictated he should go inside and give her some privacy. But he had an uneasy feeling about the situation and he'd learned to trust his instincts. So he leaned back against the building, keeping his eyes fixed on the pair.

He planned to stay out of it, truly he did. But

when she raised her voice and the man in the dark suit grabbed her arm, Josh was down the street and at her side in a heartbeat.

"Get your hands off her," he growled. Brother or not, no man was going to raise a hand to Stacie. Not if Josh had anything to say about it.

The man whirled, releasing his hold on her arm, his lips thinning with displeasure.

Even if Josh hadn't known this was Stacie's brother, the resemblance between the two would have given it away. Although Paul was a good head taller than his sister and his hair a shade lighter, their almond-shaped eyes and patrician noses proclaimed them family.

"I don't know how it is where you come from," Josh said, "but around here we don't manhandle a woman."

Paul's gaze narrowed and Stacie took a step away, the action bringing her closer to Josh. It seemed natural for him to slip an arm around her shoulder, but she shrugged off the support, making it clear this was *her* battle.

A mocking little smile lifted her brother's lips. He shifted his gaze to Stacie. "Tell me you're not walking away from the opportunity of a lifetime for a two-bit cowboy."

"He's not why I said no," Stacie said in a calm voice. "Josh is an acquaintance, not a boyfriend."

Josh bristled. Acquaintance? He was *acquainted* with the librarian in town, but he'd never held her in his arms. Or felt her lips against his.

"Then this stubborn refusal of yours makes no sense." Paul's gaze remained fixed on Stacie. "Why would you turn down such a terrific offer?"

"That's what I've been trying to tell you," Stacie said. "But you just keep cutting me off."

Josh hid a smile. He'd only known Stacie a short time, but even he knew she was no pushover.

Paul crossed his arms. "I'm listening now."

Though his body language didn't indicate a willingness to consider any position other than his own, his tone was somewhat conciliatory. It must have been enough, because the tension left Stacie's shoulders and a glimmer of hope filled her eyes.

"I've never wanted to work in corporate America," she said in a soft voice. "It's just not me."

"You have a degree in business." Paul's entire attention was on his sister. "This position will allow you to not only use your education, but also be close to us."

Stacie opened her mouth but Paul continued without taking a breath.

"You don't even have to interview," Paul said. "The CEO is a friend and he's willing to hire you based on my recommendation."

"Paul—" Stacie raised a hand, but her brother was on a roll and seemed determined to finish.

"Best of all—since you're unemployed, you can start next week." He patted he suit coat pocket. "I have two return tickets. You can be back home tomorrow."

Stacie...leaving? An icy chill gripped Josh's heart.

"I'm not moving back to Ann Arbor." Stacie's chin lifted in a stubborn tilt. "Not tomorrow. Not in a week, a month or a year."

To Josh's surprise, Paul didn't immediately reply. Instead, his gaze searched Stacie's face for a long moment.

"I don't understand you," he said, his voice heavy with disappointment. "You have friends back home who miss you. Family that misses you. And now a great job handed to you on a silver platter. Why won't you at least consider coming back?"

Despite his heavy-handed methods, the man came across as sincere and made some good points. But when Josh glanced at Stacie, she didn't appear swayed.

"How many times do I have to tell you? I don't want to be stuck behind a desk." Her eyes flashed and Josh swore he saw steam coming from her nose. She reminded Josh of a bull ready to charge. "I only majored in business because Daddy insisted."

"Dad wants you to have a good life. A secure future." Paul's tone made it clear he agreed. "He loves you, Stacie. We all do. And we're worried about you."

Stacie raised a brow.

"Okay, *I'm* the one who's worried." Paul's voice broke. He took a moment to regain his composure before casting a sideways glance at Josh. "Send the cowboy back to the ranch. This is family business."

Though listening to their intimate conversation certainly wasn't his idea of fun, Josh kept his feet planted. He'd leave, but only if Stacie asked.

"He stays," Stacie said firmly.

Paul closed his eyes and blew out a hard breath.

"Mom and Dad have always wanted what's best for you," Paul repeated, once again sounding surprisingly sincere. "We all want that."

Stacie took a step forward and rested a hand on Paul's arm. "The problem is what you think is best for me is not what *I* want."

Anger flared in Paul's eyes. "What is it you want to do, little sister? Spend your life walking other people's dogs? Making lattes in a coffee shop? Or maybe you want to marry a cowboy and live in the middle of nowhere?"

Stacie's hand jerked back and her cheeks pinked as if she'd been slapped. But if her brother thought that harsh words and bullying tactics were the answer, all Paul had to do was look in her eyes to see that he'd lost any ground he might have gained.

"I don't care what you think of my choices, Paul." Her voice was icy cold, a stark contrast to her brother's heated passion. "Just because I have different goals, other things I want out of life…"

Paul's lips pressed together and he appeared to be fighting for control. "You and Amber Turlington, always searching for your damned bliss."

The words sounded like a curse. Still, Stacie couldn't help but smile at the familiar name. She and Amber had been best friends all through school. "Amber and I used to joke that we were twins separated at birth."

"She was never happy in Ann Arbor, either," Paul

said, a surprising bitterness in his tone. "She always wanted something more. And look where it got her."

"Where it got her?" Stacie's voice rose. She couldn't believe his arrogance. "The school where she's teaching in Los Angeles may not be nationally acclaimed, and she may not be making the big bucks, but every day she makes a difference in the lives of her students."

"You haven't heard." It was a statement, not a question. The bleak look in Paul's eyes sent a shiver of unease up Stacie's spine.

"Heard what?" She knew Amber and Paul kept in touch. A long time ago Paul had desperately wanted to marry her friend. Though he'd moved on and married another woman, Stacie knew Amber still held a special spot in his heart.

A tiny muscle in Paul's jaw jumped. "I thought Karen and you would have talked by now."

Karen was one of Stacie's sisters. She'd left a handful of messages the past week, but Stacie hadn't gotten around to calling her back. "Karen and I haven't connected. Did she hear from Amber?"

"Amber is dead." The muscle in Paul's jaw began twitching. "Some punk shot her in the school parking lot."

His words seemed to come from far away. Stacie turned hot and then cold. A vision of Amber— auburn hair, bright green eyes and an ever-present smile—flashed before her. How could her friend be dead? She'd been the most alive person Stacie knew.

"It's not true." Stacie shook her head, trying to

dispel the picture of Amber lying in her own blood. "You're making it up. You want me to move back. To give up my dreams. Just like you wanted Amber to give up her dream for you. But she didn't and I won't—"

"Shh. It's okay." Josh moved to her side and this time when he placed a steadying arm around her shoulders, she didn't resist.

"The funeral was Thursday," Paul said, sounding incredibly weary.

Stacie swallowed a sob. It seemed easier to focus on her anger, rather than the pain tearing her heart in two.

"Why didn't you tell me?" Her voice sounded shrill even to her own ears. "I'd have come. She was my friend. My best friend."

"Karen and I both left messages asking you to call us back," Paul said simply. "I couldn't leave that news on voice mail."

Regret mixed with shame washed over Stacie. She leaned against Josh, drawing strength from his support. She'd been wrong to blame Paul. It was her fault for not calling back. She'd put off dialing his number for one reason: every time she talked to him or Karen, she hung up feeling like a big failure. Now Amber's parents probably thought she didn't care enough to come back for the funeral. "I can't imagine how hard this is on her family."

"I know exactly how they're feeling," Paul said.

"That's why I'm here. I love you, Stacie. I want to make sure what happened to Amber doesn't happen to you."

Midmorning sun streamed through the lace curtains of the kitchen window and the heavenly aroma of freshly brewed coffee filled the air. Stacie stared down at her steaming cup of French roast, still unsettled by last night's events.

She lifted her gaze to find Lauren and Anna staring, waiting for her to finish the story. "I convinced Josh that my brother could see me safely home. Paul and I spent a couple of hours talking…crying…talking some more. He slept for three or four hours then headed back to Billings to catch his flight."

Though she and Paul disagreed on most issues, they'd both loved Amber. Stacie felt tears sting the back of her lids, but she blinked them back. She'd never liked crying in public. Even if in this case the "public" were her close friends.

Anna, sponge in hand, interrupted her counter cleaning to eye Stacie with a thoughtful look. "I'm still confused. Your brother wanted you to move home because a high school friend of yours died. I don't get it."

"I do." Lauren took a dainty bite of her egg sandwich. "Amber was looking for her bliss and she died. Stacie is doing the same and Paul is worried something may happen to her."

"That doesn't make any sense." Anna took a

swipe at the kitchen counter. "Stacie's in Montana, not big, bad L.A."

"Her brother lost someone he loved." Lauren tapped a finger on the tabletop. "When Stacie didn't return his calls, he panicked, thinking something may have happened to her, too."

"I think he knows better now," Stacie said with a dry chuckle. Heck, if she didn't laugh she was going to cry. "How many women have their own watch-dog?"

Lauren shot her a questioning glance.

"Josh came searching for me," Stacie explained. "He wasn't sure Paul was trustworthy."

Anna smiled. "Welcome to the cowboy world, where men think all women need to be protected."

"It was sweet," Stacie admitted, "considering we barely know each other."

Lauren choked on her sandwich and Anna let loose a very unladylike snort.

Stacie pulled her brows together. "What is it with you guys?"

"Puh-leeze," Lauren said. "I saw how you two were looking at each other, how close he was holding you on the dance floor. I couldn't have asked for a better advertisement for the survey unless you were naked and getting it on."

"Oh my God, Lauren," Anna's peal of laughter rang throughout the room, "you are so bad."

Stacie took a sip of coffee, even as her cheeks heated. "Well, anyway, that was our last date."

"Why?" Anna asked. "I saw real chemistry."

"Lots of chemistry," Lauren added, an impish smile on her lips.

Stacie ignored the good-natured teasing. "Josh and I decided on the first date that we weren't—" Stacie paused. To say that they weren't a good match might be a slap in the face to Lauren's survey. "That while we get along great, we don't want the same things out of life. Sort of like Amber and Paul."

"I could put you back in the system," Lauren volunteered. "Match you again."

Stacie shook her head. Talking to Paul about her dreams had only reinforced her desire to find her bliss. While Paul thought hearing about Amber would make her run back to Ann Arbor, the story had the opposite effect.

Regardless of what her brother thought, Amber had been happy in L.A. in a way she'd never have been happy in Ann Arbor. Just like Stacie would never be happy until she found her purpose in life.

Surprisingly Lauren didn't try to change Stacie's mind. Instead she forked a bite of coffee cake. "Remind me to give you the postmatch survey after church."

"You're going to church?" Anna's blue eyes sparkled. "After the comment you made about Stacie and Josh on the dance floor?"

"It's her penance," Stacie said, unable to keep her blood from heating at the thought of her and Josh on the hardwood…naked.

"I promised Pastor Barbee we'd be there and I'm

a woman of my word," Lauren said, suddenly all prim and proper. "Service starts at eleven."

"Count me out." Anna sat back in her chair. "I need a breather from the Sweet River folks."

"Don't give me that," Lauren said. "Every time I saw you last night you were smiling."

"I had an okay time," Anna admitted. "But I grew up here. I know what this place is like, and I'm not going to let them suck me back into the fold. Self-preservation dictates I keep my distance."

"Me, too," Stacie said, knowing if she didn't she might end up with a naked cowboy in her bed.

"Well, you can both start keeping your distance... tomorrow," Lauren declared. "The church is having a box-lunch fund-raiser after the service and we're participating."

Chapter Six

The sun shone brightly overhead and the temperature was a balmy seventy-five when Josh joined the citizens of Sweet River on the back lawn of the First Congregational Church.

He'd stayed at the dance way too late last night. Then, when he finally got back to the ranch, sleep had eluded him.

It seemed as if he'd just drifted off when the alarm sounded. He'd been tempted to stay home and do some scraping on the house. But he'd promised Pastor Barbee he'd participate in the box-lunch auction.

The once-a-year event benefited the church's Vacation Bible School program, and the coffers desperately needed replenishing. Last year the weather had been bad and the turnout dismal.

In the tradition of the Wild West, single women made up a picnic lunch for two and bachelors bid on the decorated baskets of food.

Two years ago Josh ended up having lunch with Caroline Carstens, who'd been back from college for the summer. It had been pure torture. She'd spent the entire lunch talking about her fancy cell phone and her blog. Not his style at all. This year had to be better. If only Stacie were participating…

As quickly as the thought entered his mind, he dropkicked it out of his head. They'd gone to the dance together only as a favor to Lauren. There was no reason for them to spend any more time together.

The auction had already started by the time Josh took a seat on the grassy knoll. The minister—who supplemented his church income by being an auctioneer—was holding up a basket with sunflowers on the side. Josh immediately recognized it. He kept his mouth shut and his hand down. A guy could only take so much, even if it did benefit the church.

The basket was won by the younger brother of one of Josh's friends. He let out a war whoop when the minister pointed to Caroline.

There were only a handful of baskets left when Stacie and her roommates arrived and deposited theirs at the minister's feet.

A murmur went through the crowd and the bidding grew spirited when first Lauren's and then Anna's were brought to the stage. Stacie's was the next one up.

There were many guys who hadn't yet bid, including Wes Danker. Josh wondered which would have the pleasure of Stacie's company.

Pastor Barbee began his spiel, but instead of men shouting out bids, there was only silence.

The minister tapped the microphone, making sure it was still on. "Let's start with twenty-five. Who'll give twenty-five?"

No one said a word, much less called out a bid. A hush settled over the crowd. Stacie's cheeks turned bright pink.

When Wes turned and cast a pointed glance at him, Josh finally realized what was up. In the minds of the citizens of Sweet River, Stacie was his girl and they weren't about to poach.

But Stacie wouldn't know that. All she knew was that no one wanted to have lunch with her.

Though Josh had vowed to keep his distance, he refused to see her humiliated. He stood. "One hundred dollars."

Okay, so that was overkill. With no one bidding against him he could have had her basket for five. But how would that have looked to Stacie and to the town? Like he didn't value her company. Anyway, that's how it would appear...

A look of relief crossed the minister's face. "Number fifteen sold to Joshua Collins for one hundred dollars."

Stacie turned, looking utterly delectable in a pink-and-white summer dress. He couldn't read her expression from the distance, but she lifted her hand in a little wave.

The remaining picnic lunches went quickly. It was soon time for Josh to claim his basket…and Stacie.

He moved to the front and grabbed the wicker handle before turning to face the pretty brunette. Josh shifted from one foot to the other, feeling as awkward as a new colt. "Together again."

"So it seems."

He noticed her eyes were red rimmed and he remembered the look on her face last night when she'd learned her friend had been murdered. "Look," he said. "We don't have to do this."

"I think we do." A slight smile lifted Stacie's lips. "You saved me from owning the only basket not bid on."

"It wasn't you," he said. "Or your basket."

A doubtful look crossed her face. "What else could it be?"

Out of the corner of his eye he saw the pastor's wife headed their way. To be interrogated—no matter how well-meaning—was the last thing Stacie needed after her emotional night.

"Walk with me." He cupped her elbow in his hand and started back in the direction of where he'd been sitting. They quickly reached the spot, but Josh didn't slow his pace. "You've been marked as mine and guys 'round here don't trespass."

A look of startled surprise crossed her face and she stopped. "Seriously?"

"I know." He placed his hand against the small of

her back and urged her across the street toward a small park surrounded by an ornate wrought-iron fence. "Sounds crazy, but…"

Josh didn't know what else to say. While in many places a pretty woman was always considered fair game, that wasn't the Sweet River way.

"I think it's admirable," Stacie said. "You don't see loyalty like that anymore."

This time Josh was the one surprised. "I thought you'd be angry."

A tiny frown marred Stacie's forehead. "Why?"

"For starters," Josh said, "I messed up your chance to meet and have lunch with someone new."

"I didn't want to eat with anyone else," Stacie said in a matter-of-fact tone.

His heart skipped a beat. "You didn't—er…don't?"

"What's the point? Most guys are looking for a wife." She reached over and gave his hand a quick squeeze. "You and I know exactly where the other stands."

The realization should have made him happy. Instead a leaden weight filled his stomach.

Stacie took the basket from his hands and placed it on a nearby picnic table. She flipped the top open and pulled out a tablecloth. "I hope you're in the mood to experiment."

He spread out the blue-and-white cloth while she took out a bottle of wine and two glasses. "Experiment?"

Stacie gestured toward the basket. "The food I packed isn't ordinary picnic fare."

"I like out of the ordinary," Josh said, realizing with sudden shock that it was true. Stacie was different from any other woman he'd known, and he was starting to like the roller-coaster ride he'd been on since he met her.

"Then you're in for a treat."

Josh stared at Stacie's hazel eyes and moist red lips. "I'm sure I am."

The air, which had been light and slightly breezy only moments before, turned thick and heavy. Everything faded and the only thing Stacie was conscious of was Josh: the long, dark lashes that framed brilliant blue eyes, the firm lips that had tasted so sweet…

"What did you make?" His words were like a splash of cold water.

Stacie blinked and pulled herself back to reality—the reality that said kissing Josh the first time had been a mistake, the reality that warned kissing him a second time would only compound the error.

"I've got tomato basil and brie spread, Spanish shrimp and rice salad and raspberry crumb bars. But my absolute favorite is the gourmet tuna salad on wheat." Already anticipating the tangy blend of tuna, capers and almonds, Stacie's taste buds tingled. "Tuna is one of my favorite ingredients. The green olives and Worcestershire sauce take it from ordinary to—"

"Tuna?"

Stacie put down the silverware and napkins and gave him her full attention. "Are you feeling okay?"

"Absolutely," he said. "I'm just not a tuna man."

Of course. This was cattle country. Roast beef and Swiss would have been a safer choice. Not to mention tuna could be bland and tasteless—depending on who did the preparation. But hers was spectacular. She had no doubt that he'd be a huge fan after one bite. "You'll love mine."

"I don't think I made myself clear," Josh said. "I can't stomach the stuff."

His tone left no room for argument or doubt.

Stacie leaned forward, letting her hair swing to cover her face as she rummaged in the basket, not wanting him to see her distress. "That's okay." She told herself not to take his dislike personally. "There's plenty else to eat."

"The smell alone nauseates me," he added.

"I understand." Disappointment caused her voice to be sharper than she'd intended. She lifted her head and softened the words with a smile. "We all have foods we don't like. In fact, this reminds me of a story my mother liked to tell."

Uncorking the wine, Josh filled each glass halfway and handed one to Stacie. He took a seat on one side of the picnic table and she sat opposite him.

Josh took a sip. "Did the story involve tuna?"

Stacie laughed as she pulled out the rest of the food. "Scalloped potatoes."

His eyes lit up. "A favorite of mine."

"Mine, too," Stacie said. "Pretty much every one I know likes them…except my mother. She got sick after eating a big helping one year. After that, her formerly favorite casserole shot straight to the top of her cannot-stand-the-sight-or-smell list."

Josh grabbed a piece of French bread and scooped out a little of the basil and brie spread.

"What was weird was a couple of times every year she'd make it for my dad." Stacie could still see the look of surprise and pleasure on her father's face when he'd see the casserole dish on the table.

"Why did she do that?" Josh added a healthy helping of shrimp and rice salad to his plate. "I'm sure he didn't expect it."

"You're right. He didn't expect it at all." Stacie's lips lifted in a smile. "Whenever I asked her, she'd just laugh and say 'nothing says love like scalloped potatoes.'"

Josh paused, a piece of French bread in hand, a thoughtful look on his face. "She did it to show how much he meant to her."

Stacie took a sip of wine. "I didn't understand when I was little, but as I got older I came to that same conclusion. It was a way of saying 'I love you' without words."

"They sound like a nice couple." Josh took a bite of the French bread with spread and murmured his appreciation.

"They are," Stacie admitted. "Their only fault is an intense desire to make me more like them."

"I understand." Josh's eyes took on a distant look. "From the time I was small I was pushed toward a career in business, not ranching."

Boy, did Stacie understand what that was like.

She'd never bought into her family's rigid definition of success. And because of that, they'd always thought she was a flake.

"My dad has a successful auto dealership in Ann Arbor. My mother is a CPA with her own firm." Stacie shook her head. "My siblings all inherited that entrepreneurial spirit."

"At least you have that in common," Josh commented.

"What are you talking about?"

"Your dream is to own a catering firm," he said. "Doesn't get much more entrepreneurial than that."

"I disagree." Stacie took a bite of the shrimp and rice salad and chewed thoughtfully. "I'd be doing it because it's my passion, not because I want to make gobs of money."

"Success and passion don't have to be mutually exclusive." Josh's gaze lingered on her face. "I have to turn a profit to keep the ranch going."

"I realize that. I just don't want money to be the main focus." Stacie sighed. Sometimes it felt as if she'd never find her bliss. "At least Amber got to live out her dream."

A lump formed in her throat. Stacie glanced down at the food on her plate. Her appetite had vanished.

"Losing a good friend," Josh said in a soft, low voice, "is like losing a family member."

"She was so full of life. And such a good person." Tears filled Stacie's eyes despite her best efforts to keep them at bay. "She didn't deserve to die like that."

She dropped her fork on the brightly colored

paper plate then buried her head in her hands. Tears slipped down her cheeks.

Though she hadn't heard Josh get up he was suddenly sitting beside her. "You're right," he said. "She didn't deserve to die like that."

"I'm sorry. I thought I'd cried myself out last night." Reaching into her pocket, Stacie pulled out a tissue and blew her nose. "I just feel so empty inside."

A family spilled into the park. The kids scurried to the play equipment while the parents plopped an overflowing picnic basket on the table. The man waved to Josh and the woman cast a curious glance at Stacie.

Stacie wiped the remaining wetness from her cheeks with the tips of her fingers. "Let's go before your friends come over."

Josh's gaze searched her face, two lines of worry between his eyes. "There's a place on my ranch. I don't know if it has good cosmic energy or what, but I always feel better after I've been there. Best of all, it's completely private."

Stacie didn't think there was a single place on earth that had the power to lighten her heart. Still, going back to the house and crying in her room held little appeal. "Would you show it to me?"

"Of course," he said, his eyes never leaving hers. A slight smile lifted his lips. "Trust me—when you get there, you're going to say 'Josh Collins, you are so smart. This place is just what I needed.'"

"I suppose you'll expect a kiss, too."

She wasn't sure who was most surprised by the words, but the slow grin that spread like molasses across his face told her he liked the idea.

His gaze dropped to linger on her lips and they immediately began to tingle.

"Kissing," he said softly, "will be entirely up to you."

Chapter Seven

After dropping off the picnic basket at Anna's house and changing into a pair of jeans—at Josh's insistence—Stacie hopped into his truck.

Excitement nudged at her melancholy. But it wasn't until she rolled the window down and let the clean, fresh air rush in that a smile touched her lips. It helped that Josh continued to keep the conversation light. Time passed quickly and soon the cross timbers announcing the Double C ranch came into view.

Just as the truck turned into the long lane leading up to the house, Bert burst from a grove of trees into view. The dog ran alongside the truck, barking and wagging her tail, the entire length of the lane.

The minute the vehicle stopped, Stacie jumped

out and gave Bert a big hug, receiving a doggie kiss
on the cheek in return. When she learned Josh expected her to ride a *horse* to his mysterious location,
she almost balked. But the clouds had disappeared
and the sun now shone high in the sky. It seemed like
a sign. As did the fact that Josh gave her a mare so
gentle a three-year-old could ride her.

Brownie only had one speed: slow and easy.
Stacie liked the horse more with each plodding step.

Josh's mount, a shiny black stallion named Ace,
chomped at the bit, but Josh kept him in check. As
they left the yard, Bert and several of the puppies
came running.

They were a good ten minutes from the house
when a couple of the pups took off in another direction. Worry bubbled inside Stacie as they disappeared from the sight. "Should we go after them?"

"No need," Josh said. "Blue heelers are smart and
the young ones are old enough to do some exploring.
They'll find their way home."

Stacie cast another look at the ridge where she'd
last seen the puppies. "If you're sure…"

"Positive," he said in a reassuring tone, and she
knew he'd heard the worry in her voice. "How are
you and Brownie getting along?"

"I'm starting to feel like a real cowgirl." And that
wasn't a bad thing…as long as it was temporary.
Stacie patted the coarse brown hair on Brownie's
neck. "You're right. She *is* very gentle."

His smile held a bit of "I told you so," but the
words remained unspoken.

"I'd never put you in harm's way," he said instead.

A warmth that had nothing to do with the sun heated her body. "I appreciate that."

"You look like you're feeling a little better."

"I am." Maybe it was the sunny sky or fresh air or being with Josh…whatever the reason, the dark cloud that had hung over her head seemed to have vanished. "But I feel guilty for enjoying the day."

"Why would you feel guilty?"

Stacie urged Brownie across a trickle of water too small to be called a stream. "Amber hasn't even been dead two weeks. Yet for the past hour I've hardly thought of her."

Josh nodded and she could see the sympathy in his eyes. They rode in silence for several minutes before he turned in his saddle. "When I was twelve, my grandfather died. I thought my life had come to an end." Sadness underscored his words. "Granddad loved ranching. He taught me how to rope and ride and most of all to respect the land."

"You must miss him very much." The sentiment seemed inadequate, considering Josh had not only lost a grandfather but a *mentor.*

"At first, a lot," he agreed. "Then one day I realized I hadn't thought of him in over a week. Like you, I felt guilty. Until my father pointed something out to me."

"What was that?"

"There was no chance I'd forget Granddad." A smile lifted the corners of his lips. "He's as much a part of me as this land. Whenever I rope a cow or string a line of fence I think of him. He'll be with me forever. Just like your friend Amber. The memories you shared will always be a part of you."

A flood of gratitude washed over Stacie. Somehow Josh had managed to articulate her fears and worries and give her comfort without making her feel stupid. She paused, searching for words that would convey her appreciation for his compassion without being gushy.

Josh gave an embarrassed laugh, obviously misinterpreting her silence. "I usually don't talk this much."

Without giving her a chance to reassure him, he kicked his heels and Ace climbed the hill in front of them, stopping at the top.

Stacie stared at Josh's back and waited for her horse to follow. When Brownie didn't move, Stacie lightly tapped the mare's sides with her heels. The horse still didn't budge.

Suddenly a series of whistles split the air. Out of the corner of her eye Stacie saw Bert shoot from the bushes and head straight for Brownie's rear hoofs. Seconds later, the gentle brown beauty stepped forward, methodically making her way to the top. Every time the horse's pace slowed, Bert barked encouragement.

Once Brownie stood by Ace, Bert disappeared again. Seemingly mesmerized by the view, Josh didn't even glance her way.

Stacie released the reins and stretched, reveling in the feel of the sun against her face. She'd spent the last ten years in Denver, surrounded by tall buildings and masses of people. And she'd loved every minute.

But now, breathing in the clean, fresh air and gazing at the green and amber-colored grass that stretched like a patchwork quilt all the way to mountains in the distance, she could understand why Josh liked it. A sense of peace stole over her. "Breathtaking."

"It is." Josh's gaze lingered for a long moment on the valley before shifting back to Stacie. "But this isn't our final destination. To get *there,* we need to walk."

He slipped off his horse with well-practiced ease and then helped Stacie off Brownie.

"What about the horses?" she asked. "We can't just leave them here."

"Bert will watch them." Josh's piercing whistle split the air again and the dog came running.

"It's not far." Josh took her arm as he led her down a dirt path. "Watch out for the poison ivy and…" He cleared his throat. "Just stay on the path and you'll be fine."

Stacie couldn't remember if poison ivy had three leaves or four, and she had no idea what else she should avoid. But as she continued to walk, she decided she didn't need to know as long as she kept her feet on the path.

Several black-headed birds circled overhead and the leaves of a large cottonwood rustled in the light breeze, but other than the music of nature, silence surrounded them. Grinning at the fanciful thoughts, Stacie followed Josh down the narrow path.

"This is it." He stopped and stepped to the side, making room for her.

While the view from where they'd left the horses had been amazing, this scenery stole her breath. Miles of bluebells blanketed the meadow below. Off to the right, next to a bubbling brook, a herd of cattle grazed on a carpet of green grass.

"Yours?" she asked, her mind too full to form a more coherent question.

His arms spread out. "As far as the eye can see."

"Unbelievable."

"I hoped you'd like it."

"It doesn't seem like something that could be owned." Stacie struggled to bring her tangled thoughts into some semblance of order. She lifted her gaze to the bright blue expanse. "Any more than one person could claim the sky."

A look she couldn't immediately identify flashed across his face, and she feared he'd taken offense.

She placed a hand on his arm. "I'm not saying this *isn't* yours, just that—"

"No worries." Josh reached up and covered her hand with his. "I've had those same thoughts."

"Really?"

He nodded. "My ancestors settled here in the 1800s. While the deed says I own these acres, I see myself more as a caretaker. My job is to make sure the land will be here, unspoiled, for generations to come."

"For your children," Stacie said. "And their children."

"For them and anyone else." A smile lifted Josh's lips. "You don't have to own a piece of land to appreciate its beauty."

Stacie thought of the vacations her family had taken when she was growing up. There had been so many states, so many places that had filled her with awe. Places she'd like to visit again. Now she had another to add to her list.

"I'll remember this always." She turned to face him. "One day I'll return."

Josh reached out and touched her arm. The scent of jasmine filled his nostrils. Would he ever be able to smell that scent without thinking of her? "You'll always be welcome here, as well as your husband and kids."

Confusion clouded her gaze. "Husband?"

"By the time you get back to Montana, you'll likely be married," he said in as offhand a tone as he could muster. "Probably even have a couple children in tow."

Though his voice gave nothing away, the thought burned like a branding iron to his heart and suddenly he knew why. He wanted her to be happy, of course, but he wanted her to be happy with *him*. Not with some nameless, faceless executive who wouldn't know how to nourish her soul.

Nourish her soul? Dear God, he sounded like one of the valentines Sharon's Food Mart sold every year.

As far as him nourishing Stacie's soul, that, too, was laughable. He hadn't been able to meet Kristin's needs so what made him think he could do so for Stacie?

"That's a ways off." Her eyes took on a faraway look. "There's so much I want to do, so many things I want to accomplish first, beginning with finding my bliss."

"You'll find it," he said. "Then you'll meet someone, fall in love—"

"I can see that happening more to you than to me," she said, an odd look on her face.

"Don't think so." Josh gave a little laugh. "Been there. Done that. Didn't work."

"You were married?"

The shock in her voice took him by surprise. He'd thought Anna had told her.

"I was."

"Does she live in Sweet River?" Stacie asked, and though her tone was casual, he could see the curiosity in her gaze. "Do you have any children?"

"She moved to Kansas City after the divorce." He kept his tone matter-of-fact. "We were only married a couple years. Not enough time for kids."

Back then, he'd wanted a baby, but Kristin hadn't been ready. Now he was glad they hadn't had children.

Stacie touched his arm. "I'm sorry it didn't work out."

"I had my chance." Josh shrugged. "I'll probably have a series of flings and die alone."

Josh couldn't believe the thought had formed in his brain much less made it past his lips. It wasn't the way he felt…not really.

Unlike some of the men he knew, Josh liked the idea of spending his life with one woman and had always thought he'd make a good husband. Though his failure with Kristin had made him doubt himself for a while, he knew he had a lot to offer the right woman.

"You'll find someone," she said softly. Before he could respond she slipped her arms around his neck, her curves pressing against him. "Your soul mate is out there. In fact, I bet right now she's finding her way to you."

He knew he should push her away, but how could he when he liked having her close? Especially since the "soul mate" in his head had started looking and sounding an awful lot like the woman in his arms. "I don't—"

She brushed his lips with hers, silencing the protest. "Say 'Stacie, you're right. That's how it's going to be.'"

Though Josh didn't like anyone putting words in his mouth, if it would keep her close a few seconds longer, he'd agree to almost anything. "Stacie," he lowered his head and planted kisses up the side of her neck. "You're right."

She moaned and leaned her head back, exposing the soft ivory skin of her neck to his lips.

He trailed his tongue along her jaw line and heard her breath catch in her throat.

"Say 'that's how it's going to be.'" Her breathing had grown ragged, but she managed to get the words out.

"Stacie." He put his hands on her hips and pulled her so close there was no space left between them. "*This* is how it's going to be."

He closed his lips over hers and drank her in. And when she opened her mouth and her tongue fenced with his in a delicious thrust and slide, all desire to pull back fled.

He burned with the need to make her his. To make her love him…

The thought was like a bucket of water on the fire that threatened his good sense. He took a step back, dislodging her fingers from his hair, ignoring her murmured words of protest.

"On second thought, *this,*" he said, trying to contain the tremble in his voice and not completely succeeding, "is a very bad idea."

Stacie let her hands drop to her side, heartbeat pounding and her breath coming in short puffs. She struggled to pull herself together. The last thing she wanted was for him to see how much his kiss had affected her. She resisted the urge to touch her still-tingling lips.

"Beautiful scenery always affects me this way," Stacie said finally when the awkward silence lengthened. "When I was in fourth grade, our Girl Scout troop leader and her husband took a group of us to Mackinac Island. When the island came into view,

I was so excited. Unfortunately poor Mr. Jefferis was standing next to me."

Josh's eyes widened. "You kissed your troop leader's husband?"

"I was ten." She swallowed a giggle. "I gave his arm a big ole squeeze."

Josh laughed, his eyes now filled with merriment. "What am I going to do with you?"

Stacie knew what she wanted him to do. She longed to be back in his arms with his lips pressed against hers, but he was right—such intimacy *was* a bad idea. Still, the urge persisted.

She desperately needed to put some distance between them…at least until she felt more able to resist temptation. Glancing around, Stacie saw a narrow path behind him. She guessed the trail would be an alternate way back to the horses.

"Catch me." As she spoke, Stacie turned and scampered down the path, unable to resist tossing one last taunt over her shoulder. "If you can."

"Stacie, no."

She heard him call out, but didn't slow her steps. The path quickly disappeared. Soon navigating her way through the dense brush and broken tree branches took her entire attention.

She could hear Josh closing in and considered conceding, but instead she pressed forward.

"Stacie, there are snakes—"

The words had barely registered when she stepped on something soft, yet firm. A feeling of impending doom settled over her. Perhaps running off *had* been a mistake.

Then she heard a hissing sound and realized there was no "perhaps" about it.

Chapter Eight

The ominous hissing was immediately followed by a stabbing pain in her ankle. Stacie screamed and hopped back, her heart stopping at the sight of a large shiny brown snake with black blotches.

"What happened?" Josh was beside her in a heartbeat, his eyes dark with concern.

Swallowing a sob, Stacie pointed to the five-foot reptile slithering in the opposite direction. "A rattle-snake bit me."

Josh's gaze turned sharp and assessing. After a second he crouched down, gently pushing up the edge of her jeans.

"I don't feel so good." The world started to spin and darkness threatened.

"Lean over," he said, urging her head down. "Take deep breaths."

Bracing her hands on her thighs, Stacie focused on breathing in and out. After a few seconds the darkness receded.

"My ankle burns." Though her insides felt like a quivering mass of jelly, her voice came out steady.

Josh met her gaze. "I'm taking you home."

He scooped her into his arms and walked with long, purposeful strides back the way he'd come.

Though her ankle burned, it didn't stop a thrill from traveling up Stacie's spine. She'd never been carried by a man before. Never been held in such a protective embrace. It was so…Sir Galahadish.

The second they reached the clearing he gently sat her down and knelt beside her. "I'm going to take a closer look."

Stacie tried to remember what she'd learned about snakebites in the first-aid class she'd taken in college. "Are you going to cut my leg and suck out the venom?"

He looked up from his examination and audibly exhaled. "Just as I thought, it wasn't a rattler."

Though she didn't want to doubt him, the reptile had looked eerily similar to the rattlesnakes she'd once seen on Animal Planet.

"The snake you pointed out looked like a gopher," he continued. "Those snakes have similar coloring to a rattler, but the head and body are slightly different. I didn't want to assume anything until I checked the wound more carefully, but now that I've seen the fang marks, I'm positive it was a gopher snake."

His voice was strong and confident, but a few doubts lingered. "How can you be sure?"

"Rattlesnakes have fangs only on the upper jaw, so when they strike, you see only one or two puncture marks," Josh said in a matter-of-fact tone. "Gopher snakes have upper and lower fangs, so they leave two sets of holes."

Stacie steadied her nerves and glanced down. Four needlelike punctures pierced the skin. "Are gopher snakes poisonous?"

"Nope," Josh said. "No venom."

Stacie felt light-headed with relief. "I was lucky."

"You were *very* lucky."

"I shouldn't have run off like that."

"I should have told you there could be snakes in the brush," he said.

It was sweet of him to try to shoulder the blame. But she was the one who'd run into the wooded area without a second thought, and now she would endure the consequences. "My ankle still hurts a little. Is that normal?"

"I was bit once as a kid," Josh said. "I remember it hurting *a lot.*"

The words had barely left his lips when a mind-numbing pain lanced her ankle. She gasped and then pressed her lips together to keep from crying out.

Concern furrowed his brow. "C'mon." He straightened and then held out a hand. "I'll carry you back to the horses. We'll get your wound cleaned up at the house."

Though he'd carried her from where she'd been bitten, that had been a relatively short distance. The horses were farther away. "I can walk."

"No need to be brave." He laid a restraining hand on her arm.

His chin was set in a determined tilt and Stacie sensed this was an argument she was destined to lose. Still, she hesitated. "I don't want you injuring your back carrying me all that way."

"Don't worry about that." He chuckled and she was back in his arms in an instant. "I lift calves the same size as you all the time."

For a moment Stacie was taken aback, and then she had to laugh. Who but a cowboy could compare a woman to a cow and have it be charming? All the way down the path, she was acutely conscious of his broad chest and the strength in his arms. To take her mind off the pain—and him—she chattered nonstop about her aversion to snakes, mice and all things crawly.

When they reached the horses, instead of helping her mount Brownie, Josh lifted her onto Ace.

"I can ride by myself," she protested.

"You may feel faint again. I don't want you falling." His tone brooked no argument. In a matter of seconds, he sat behind her.

Stacie worried if Brownie could manage without her. But the following mare kept a brisk pace all the way to the ranch. Of course, Bert's reappearance, along with her missing puppies, may have had something to do with the mare's willingness to keep moving.

By the time Stacie reached the house, her ankle had started to swell. After turning over the care of the horses to one of his ranch hands, Josh insisted on carrying her into the house.

This time she didn't argue. Once inside he deposited her in the recliner with the footrest up and told her to stay put. He returned seconds later with a glass of water and four capsules.

"What are these?"

"Advil," he said. "Eight hundred milligrams. Prescription strength. It'll take the edge off."

At her questioning look, he smiled. "Remember, my mom is a nurse."

Stacie popped the capsules in her mouth and took a big drink of water. "What now?"

"You relax," he said. "I'll clean your ankle with antibacterial soap and then we'll get some ice on it."

Stacie glanced down at her injured foot. If she'd pulled on her pink goats as Josh had strongly suggested, the leather might have protected her skin. But no, she'd insisted on cute tennies without any socks.

"How about I go into the bathroom and wash up instead?" she said. "While I'm doing that, you can get the ice."

The look on his face said he wasn't sold on the idea. "What if you get light-headed?"

"I won't," she said in as strong a voice as she could muster. "I felt funny at first, but that was just the shock of it all. I'm better now."

"Are you sure?"

"Positive."

Josh disappeared into the kitchen and Stacie hobbled down the hall, doing her best to keep her weight off her right foot. By the time she reached the bathroom, her breath came in short puffs and her body started to shake. She placed both hands on the counter and inhaled deeply, willing herself to calm down.

A knock sounded at the door. "How are you doing?"

"Is it okay if I take a washcloth from the cabinet?" she asked.

"Use whatever you need."

Several minutes later, Stacie returned to the living room feeling more in control. Though the burning and aching wasn't any worse, it wasn't much better, either.

Exhausted and finally ready to be babied, she took a seat in the recliner and let Josh fuss over her. With gentle fingers, he treated the puncture wounds with a disinfectant before putting an ice pack, wrapped in a pillow case, on the swelling.

"The ice should stay on for about twenty minutes." He glanced at his watch. "Can I get you something to eat or drink?"

Stacie leaned her head back against the soft leather. Her stomach was still full from the picnic and, even if it wasn't, the thought of food wasn't at all appealing. "I'd rather you stay here and keep me company."

"Hang out with a pretty girl." Josh flashed a smile. "I can do that."

But before he could sit down the doorbell rang. He glanced at Stacie. "Wonder who that could be."

She shrugged, crossing her fingers that whoever it was wouldn't stay long. While she normally held to the motto "The more the merrier," she didn't feel like making small talk.

The bell sounded again and Josh cast a glance at Stacie. "I'll be right back. You stay put."

"Aye, aye, sir," Stacie brought two fingers to her forehead in a mock salute. "But if it's a snake at the door, don't let him in."

Though it wasn't all that funny, Josh laughed and headed to the front door. He wasn't sure who he expected to see on the doorstep, but it certainly wasn't Wes Danker.

As usual, the big man didn't wait for an invitation. He pushed past Josh and whipped off his hat. "You are not going to believe this. The mothership has landed."

Josh had to smile. The last time he'd seen Wes this excited was when Sharon Jensen had started carrying Ding Dongs at the food mart. "What's up?"

"Good times, that's what." Wes paced to the door then back to Josh. "And for not just me—for you, too."

Uh-oh. In the last of Wes's mothership landings, Josh had lost several hundred dollars to the slots at Lucky Lil's in Big Timber. "C'mon, Wes. I gave it a try but I'm not into gambling, no matter how loose the slots are."

"This is no gamble, my friend," Wes said in that

loud, booming voice that was as much a part of him as his ten-gallon hat. "This is a sure deal."

Stacie straightened in the chair. Though she knew it was wrong to eavesdrop, she didn't have much choice. Wes had one of those voices that carried. In fact, she was able to make out a few words of what Josh said, as well.

From what she'd heard so far, Wes was selling something and Josh wasn't buying.

"Misty saw you at the dance last night," Wes said. "The little lady liked what she saw. Now I know you and Stacie—hey, don't even try telling me you didn't notice her."

Josh said something that Stacie couldn't make out.

"That's right." Wes's booming voice drifted into the living room. "The hot blonde with the big boobs."

Josh responded in a low voice and both men laughed.

Stacie clenched her fingers together in a fist.

"Her friend Sasha has the hots for me," Wes said, and Stacie could hear the satisfaction in his voice. "She and Misty are both working at Millstead's this summer."

Millstead. Stacie had heard the name before. After a second it came to her. It was a dude ranch south of Sweet River. Most of their summer help came from the area, but according to Anna they brought in outsiders, as well.

"The best part is the girls are just here for the

summer," Wes continued. "We can hook up, have some fun and if we get tired of 'em, it's *adios* in September."

Irritation shot up Stacie's spine. She couldn't believe Wes had stopped over on a Sunday night to fix Josh up. Had the big man forgotten his friend had already been matched? She ignored the tiny voice in her head reminding her that Josh was a free agent. That he'd only taken her to the dance because of pressure from Seth. That he'd only bid on her basket because no one else would—

Stacie shoved the thoughts aside and concentrated. Despite sitting in absolute silence, she could only hear a mumbled response. She cursed the ice pack on her ankle. Only a few feet closer and she'd be able to hear every word.

"I'm headed over there now," Wes said. "Want to come along?"

Once again, Stacie heard only mumbling. But when the door closed and Josh returned to the living room without Wes, she exhaled the breath she didn't realize she'd been holding.

"How are you feeling?" he asked. "Do you need more ice?"

She shook her head. "Who was at the door?"

"Wes." Josh waved a dismissive hand. "He wanted to hang out."

"You turned him down?" Somehow Stacie managed to keep her voice casual and offhand.

"Of course." He flashed a smile. "I wanted to stay home and take care of you."

Stacie searched his eyes. Though Josh hadn't gone with the big guy tonight, that didn't mean he wouldn't be joining him another time.

But there was no answer to her unspoken question in his liquid blue depths, only concern...for her.

Warmth spread up her spine. Josh was a good man. Caring, smart and handsome to boot. The thought of him in another woman's arms set her teeth on edge.

"Stacie." His voice broke through her thoughts. "Are you okay?"

She blinked.

He moved to her side and crouched down, placing a hand on her leg, his brows pulled together in concern. "You have a funny look on your face. Is your foot hurting more?"

She stared at the face some lucky woman would one day love. A man *she* could find so easy to love.

A smart woman would let Josh take up with Misty, the dude-ranch girl. A smart woman would realize that such an action would mean someone's heart might be broken at the end of the summer, but at least it wouldn't be hers. A smart woman would never consider voicing the shocking proposal pushing against her lips.

Yet when Stacie opened her mouth, she knew she was headed down a path far more dangerous than the one she'd been on earlier. "I heard what Wes asked you."

Surprise skittered across his face. "I hope you know that—"

"I have my own proposition for you." She spoke quickly before she lost her nerve.

He cocked his head.

"If you're in the mood for a fling," she said. "Have one with me."

Chapter Nine

Josh had once been thrown off a bull and had the air knocked out of him. He felt the same way now. Had Stacie really said she was up for a no-strings-attached fling? With *him?* "Beg pardon?"

A sexy little smile lifted the corners of her smooth, soft lips. "We might as well start now."

Dropping his gaze from her mouth to the soft curves visible beneath her pink shirt, Josh processed the request. His mouth went dry imagining how her breasts would feel cradled in his work-hardened hands…how they would taste to his exploring tongue. He went instantly hard.

Though his body had made its answer clear, he'd never done his thinking with that particular part of his anatomy, and he wasn't about to start now.

Just say no, his head urged. He opened his mouth, but the simple word wouldn't come.

"Josh?" A hint of uncertainty—at total odds with her bold offer—crossed Stacie's beautiful face.

He knew he was crazy to hesitate. But for him, being intimate had never been simply about scratching an itch. When he made love to a woman, it was, well, because he cared.

But as his gaze lingered on Stacie, he realized he did care. And if he didn't take her up on her offer, any number of men would happily volunteer to take his place, including his buddy Wes Danker.

For a second, Josh saw red. Friend or not, no other man in Sweet River was going to touch Stacie. Suddenly it became clear to Josh what his answer would be, what it *had* to be.

He took her hand and stared into those beautiful hazel eyes.

"Okay." Even as Josh prayed he wouldn't regret the decision, his heart picked up speed. "Let's fling."

As Josh lowered his bedroom window shade, a frisson of excitement skittered up Stacie's spine and her heart fluttered like a trapped butterfly in her throat. With one simple comment her life had gone from slow—and slightly boring—to runaway-train mode.

She'd asked. He'd accepted. And his burning gaze told her they'd both be naked before another fifteen minutes had passed.

It's just sex, she told herself, *nothing you can't handle.*

Josh turned, his eyes dark and penetrating. "How's the ankle?"

"Good." Which was true as long as she didn't stand on it or move it much. Fortunately, she wasn't planning on being upright too much longer.

He smiled and stepped closer, his eyes filled with anticipation. She wondered how long it'd be until those beautiful eyes filled with disappointment. "Before we get started, I have a confession."

"Sounds…interesting."

Stacie twirled a piece of hair around one finger. When she'd impulsively made her offer, she'd been so caught up in the moment she'd forgotten one very important fact. "I'm not a good lover."

Despite the look of startled surprise on his face, she pressed forward. "I'm a dud in bed. I don't have much experience. And, well, I'm easily distracted."

He moved closer until he stood directly in front of her, the spicy scent of his cologne wafting in the air. "By…?"

She'd never realized before that his eyes had little gold flecks in the blue. Or that his lashes were so long that—

"What are you distracted by?" he repeated.

Right now it was by his nearness, but that wasn't the answer. Stacie could feel her face warm. She'd only wanted to alert him not to expect too much, not get into a lengthy discussion on her sexual inadequacies.

"Usually food," she said, when he continued to stare expectantly.

"You like to eat when you're making love?" He sounded interested, rather than shocked.

"No, silly," she said. "I plan menus."

"After?"

Heat rose up her neck. "During."

His mouth dropped open. "Who were these guys?" He wanted names?

"Obviously they weren't doing their job if you could plan menus while they were making love to you," he continued.

Making love? Those words were way too strong for a quick fling. "You think having sex is a job?"

"A man's 'job' is to give pleasure to his partner," Josh said. "Trust me. The only thing you're going to be thinking of tonight is how good it feels when we're together."

Doubt must have shown on her face because he chuckled softly. "Guess I'm going to have to convince you."

He pulled off his shirt and tossed it to the floor. Dear God, he was gorgeous. Broad shoulders tapering to narrow hips. Perfectly sculpted chest with a dusting of dark hair.

Every muscle and hard plane was in perfect balance. His wasn't a body toned from regular workouts in a gym, but one hardened from physical labor.

Too bad he wouldn't find her quite so perfect. Her B cups were hardly centerfold material, and while her belly was flat, the only six-pack to be found was in her refrigerator. With trembling fingers Stacie reached for the buttons on her shirt, hoping he wouldn't be too disappointed.

Before she could get the second button released, his hand closed over hers.

"No rush," he said in a deep sexy voice that sent blood flowing through her veins like warm honey. "Fast is fine, but slow is even better."

His fingers were slightly rough, and Stacie found herself wondering what those callused hands would feel like against her breasts.

That was her last coherent thought as he sat beside her and his mouth closed over hers. He caressed her skin with that mouth, planting gentle kisses on her lips, her jaw and down her neck while his hands remained respectfully on her shoulders.

He nibbled her earlobe and then moved back to her tingling lips. She opened her mouth, and when he still didn't deepen the kiss, she slid her tongue into his mouth.

His body shook and for a second she couldn't figure out why. Until she realized he was *laughing*.

She jerked back. "What is so funny?"

His lips twitched. "For two people who wanted to take things slow, we seem determined to move quickly."

"Not you." Stacie's peevish tone reflected her pent-up frustration. "You could take all night."

Josh didn't seem to take offense. In fact, his lips widened in a smile and satisfaction filled his eyes. "Sounds like I'm doing my job."

"What are you talking about?"

"Tell me honestly, have you been thinking of recipes while we've been kissing?"

"No," Stacie shot back. "I've been too busy trying to figure out how to get your tongue in my mouth and your hands on my breasts."

Heat flared in his eyes.

"I like a woman who asks for what she wants." He pushed her gently back on the bed, his fingers moving to the buttons on her shirt, even as his mouth briefly covered hers again. "And I like you."

The words were as slow and unhurried as his touch. Though her body clamored for skin-to-skin action, the knowledge that he wouldn't go too fast and leave her struggling to keep up brought a comforting warmth.

Josh had promised he would make it good for her, and though she hadn't known him long, she believed him to be a man of his word.

When his hand finally closed over her breast and his tongue slid into her mouth, an unfamiliar ache made further analytic thought impossible. And when her clothes joined his on the floor, want became need.

For the rest of the night her world was Josh, and all that mattered was him…and her…and becoming one.

Josh rolled over, the early-morning sun pulling him from his slumber. Most days he was outside before dawn, but today chores could wait. Feeling satiated and content, he stretched, reluctant to let go of the dream that had been last night.

The night had been mind-blowing. They'd tossed aside rational thought and inhibitions and never looked back.

Sensing Stacie stirring, Josh opened his eyes. Surprise shot through him at the sight of his lover propped on one elbow facing him, her dark hair tumbled around her face, her expression way too serious. And considering how late they'd been up, she looked amazingly wide-awake.

"Do you have any regrets?" she asked before he could say good morning.

"There are lots of things I regret." Josh raised himself on his elbows. "Do you have something specific in mind?"

"This," she said. "You. Me. Together. Naked."

After his enthusiasm last night, he couldn't believe she had to ask. But from her serious expression, the answer was clearly important to her.

"No," he said honestly. "Not a single regret."

"Interesting." She sat abruptly up, ignoring the sheet that fell to pool at her waist. "That's how I feel, too."

Josh told himself they were *talking,* which meant his attention should be focused on her face. Unfortunately his eyes seemed to have minds of their own. His gaze caressed her luscious curves. He'd explored every inch of her body, but seeing her in the morning light filled him with awe.

As if she could read his mind, a tiny smile lifted

her lips and she leaned forward, brushing her mouth against his. "You're the sexiest cowboy I've ever met. Not to mention an amazing lover."

He'd been determined to make their lovemaking as good for her as it was for him. It sounded as if he'd succeeded. Puffing with pride, he shot her a wink. "I promised I'd make you forget about those recipes."

Stacie laughed, her cheeks a dusky pink. "You did indeed."

He trailed a finger down the silky softness of her cheek. "It was easy. You made it easy."

He pressed his lips shut before he could tell her it was easy because of how she made him feel. But his emotions were his problem—his issue—to deal with, not hers.

She shifted again and slid the fingers of one hand through his hair, kissing the corners of his mouth. "Are you sure you don't have any more?"

He inhaled the intoxicating scent of jasmine. "More?"

"Condoms."

His body, which had soared to a heightened state of readiness, plummeted as he remembered the handful he'd found forgotten in a drawer had all been used last night. "Out."

"I wish I'd stayed on the Pill," Stacie said with a sigh. "But there was no need and—"

"There are other ways to have fun," Josh said, "that don't carry a risk of pregnancy."

"Like riding horses? Or playing with Bert?"

The innocent look on her face didn't fool him in the least. He laughed aloud. "I was thinking of more…intimate activities."

"I have a friend back in Denver." Stacie's eyes brightened. "She and her boyfriend are into role-playing. I remember one time he pretended to pick her up at the bar. She played the part of a small-town girl in the big city for the first time. I always thought the game sounded like fun."

Josh had never been much of an actor, but the last thing he wanted to do was stifle Stacie's enthusiasm. Or let her thoughts return to planning menus.

The first time they'd made love, she'd been unsure, hesitant in her overtures. Until he'd shown by his actions and his response that he was open to anything she wanted to try. And now it appeared "anything" included role-playing.

"What exactly do you have in mind?" He did his best to inject enthusiasm into his voice.

She brought a finger to her lips. "First we get dressed—"

"Get dressed?"

"Hear me out." She pulled the sheet up, covering her breasts. Apparently she really did want him to listen. "Once we have our clothes on, I go downstairs and start breakfast."

The game was sounding less appealing by the minute. But her enthusiasm continued to build, so he forced an interested expression and offered an encouraging smile. "Then what?"

"You knock on the door and we pretend we're

meeting for the first time," she said. "But with one important difference."

Josh prayed the difference was a big one, because so far this game didn't have much to recommend it. Other than, of course, it made Stacie smile.

"Have you ever been out and met someone so hot you wanted to forego the social niceties and jump him—er, her?"

He paused, remembering the moment he'd first seen Stacie on Anna's porch. "Yes, I have."

"Me, too," she said.

Josh's stomach clenched with jealousy that was as unexpected as it was ridiculous.

"When I saw you, I felt that way," she said softly. "You were so incredibly hot."

It was a nice compliment, but he hadn't forgot how she'd shot him down. "You were disappointed I was a cowboy."

She smiled. "I still thought you were sexy."

"Let me get this straight. I come to the door. I make my move and—"

"I'm ready and willing." She smiled. "But no condoms mean pants stay on."

Even with the restrictions, he could see the possibilities. "I like this game."

She lifted a brow. "Meet downstairs in twenty?"

Anticipation fueled his smile. "It's a plan."

Chapter Ten

Stacie stood at the stove in Josh's kitchen, finding it hard to stand still. She couldn't believe she'd brought up this role-playing stuff and gotten Josh to agree to it.

"Ask and it shall be given you." Though the Bible verse from last Sunday's sermon certainly wasn't intended for this situation, being bold *had* worked. Anticipation skittered up her spine.

Everything was in readiness. Coffee perked noisily in the shiny chrome pot, perfectly cooked bacon sat draining on paper towels, and the scrambled eggs were almost done when a knock sounded at the kitchen door.

Setting the burner heat to low, Stacie sauntered to the door, her heart tripping over itself. With suddenly sweaty palms, she opened the door.

"Hello, ma'am." Josh whipped off his hat. "I'm Josh Collins."

She extended her hand. "Stacie Summers. Pleased to meet you."

"Pleasure is all mine." He held her hand for several extra beats and a tingling traveled up her arm.

She took a steadying breath and motioned him inside. Instead of sitting at the table as she expected, he stepped close, crowding her.

"Are you hungry?" she stammered. Her body thrummed at his closeness.

His gaze met hers and she shivered at the hunger in the blue depths.

"Starved," he said in a deep, sexy voice that brought to mind tangled sheets and sweat-soaked bodies.

"Me, too." She moistened her lips with the tip of her tongue. "I'm ravenous."

He reached for her, but Stacie slipped past him, feeling his eyes on her as she walked to the stove. No need to make this too easy or quick. She'd discovered last night that anticipation was half the fun.

She'd just turned off the burner and scooped the eggs onto two plates when she felt his arms slip around her waist.

"It smells good in here," he said, his breath warm against her neck.

"It's the coffee." She spoke extra loud so he could hear her answer over the pounding of her heart. "I ground the beans myself."

Get 2 Books FREE!

Silhouette® Books,
publisher of women's fiction,
presents

FREE BOOKS! Use the reply card inside to get two free books!

FREE GIFTS! You'll also get two exciting surprise gifts, absolutely free!

GET 2 BOOKS

We'd like to send you two *Silhouette Special Edition*®
novels absolutely free. Accepting them puts you under
no obligation to purchase any more books.

HOW TO GET YOUR
2 FREE BOOKS AND TWO FREE GIFTS

1. Return the reply card today, and we'll send you two *Silhouette Special Edition* novels, absolutely free! We'll even pay the postage!

2. Accepting free books places you under no obligation to buy anything, ever. Whatever you decide, the free books and gifts are yours to keep, free!

3. We hope that after receiving your free books you'll want to remain a subscriber, but the choice is yours—to continue or cancel, any time at all!

EXTRA BONUS

You'll also get two free mystery gifts! (worth about $10)

® and ™ are trademarks owned and used by the trademark owner and/or its licensee.
© 2008 HARLEQUIN ENTERPRISES LIMITED.

FREE!

Return this card promptly to get
2 FREE BOOKS and 2 FREE GIFTS!

SPECIAL EDITION

YES! Please send me 2 FREE *Silhouette Special Edition®* novels, and 2 free mystery gifts as well. I understand I am under no obligation to purchase anything, as explained on the back of this insert.

335-SDL-EXAE   235-SDL-EXEQ

FIRST NAME   LAST NAME

ADDRESS

APT.#   CITY

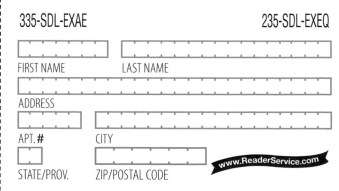

STATE/PROV.   ZIP/POSTAL CODE

Offer limited to one per household and not valid to current subscribers of Silhouette Special Edition books. Please allow 4 to 6 weeks for delivery. Offer valid while quantities last. All orders subject to approval. **Your Privacy -** Silhouette Books is committed to protecting your privacy. Our Privacy Policy is available online at www.eHarlequin.com or upon request from the Silhouette Reader Service. From time to time we make our lists of customers available to reputable third parties who may have a product or service of interest to you. If you would prefer for us not to share your name and address, please check here☐.

▼ DETACH AND MAIL CARD TODAY! ▼

(SX-SE-03/09)

www.ReaderService.com

The Silhouette Reader Service — Here's how it works:

Accepting your 2 free books and 2 free mystery gifts places you under no obligation to buy anything. You may keep the books and gifts and return the shipping statement marked "cancel". If you do not cancel, about a month later we'll send you 6 additional books and bill you just $4.24 each in the U.S. or $4.99 each in Canada. That is a savings of at least 15% off the cover price. It's quite a bargain! Shipping and handling is just 25¢ per book. You may cancel at any time, but if you choose to continue, every month we'll send you 6 more books, which you may either purchase at the discount price…or return to us and cancel your subscription.

*Terms and prices subject to change without notice. Prices do not include applicable taxes. Sales tax applicable in N.Y. Canadian residents will be charged applicable provincial taxes and GST. Offer not valid in Quebec. Credit or debit balances in a customer's account(s) may be offset by any other outstanding balance owed by or to the customer. Books received may not be as shown.

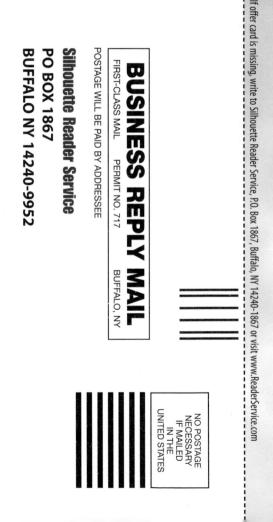

If offer card is missing, write to Silhouette Reader Service, P.O. Box 1867, Buffalo, NY 14240-1867 or visit www.ReaderService.com

BUSINESS REPLY MAIL

FIRST-CLASS MAIL   PERMIT NO. 717   BUFFALO, NY

POSTAGE WILL BE PAID BY ADDRESSEE

Silhouette Reader Service
PO BOX 1867
BUFFALO NY 14240-9952

NO POSTAGE
NECESSARY
IF MAILED
IN THE
UNITED STATES

"It's not the coffee." He leaned even closer and nuzzled her hair. "You smell like spring flowers."

"I love a man who knows how to give a compliment." She turned in his arms and faced him.

"What I want to know is," Josh's gaze dropped to her lips, "do you taste as good as you smell?"

"I—"

Josh's mouth closed over hers before she could respond. His lips began their delicious assault on her senses and Stacie forgot how to breathe. By the time he stepped back, her knees quivered like jelly and she had to lean against the counter for support.

"Yep. You *do* taste as good as you smell." His gaze dropped to her chest.

Her breasts strained against the thin cotton fabric, already anticipating the feel of his lips.

"Wow." Stacie fanned her face. "It's getting warm in here. Do you mind if I unbutton my shirt?"

His eyes glittered in the fluorescent lights of the kitchen. "Need help?"

"I'm good." Actually she was feeling more wicked than good as she unfastened each button with exaggerated slowness. Finally the shirt hung open.

"You're not wearing a bra."

"I'm not wearing any panties, either," she said, offering him an impish smile. "Course, I'm not taking off my pants."

His smile turned into a grin. "Of course you aren't."

He stepped forward, pushing aside the shirt with his fingers, his hands closing over and cradling each small mound. His thumb scrapped across the tip and Stacie moaned.

Josh lowered his head. "I have to taste—"

His mouth had just closed over one aching nipple when the door swung open with a clatter.

"The horses—" Seth pulled up short. A swath of bright red splashed across his cheeks.

Josh whirled, his muscular body shielding Stacie as she pulled her shirt together.

"Don't you knock?" Josh demanded.

"I saw the light," Seth stammered. "The guys are saddled up and ready."

"Ready for what?"

"You asked for help moving the herd this morning," Seth said.

Josh muttered an expletive and raked a hand through his hair. "I forgot."

"I understand," Seth said, his bland expression fooling no one. "You had other...things...to attend to..."

Stacie ducked her head and fastened the last button, wishing she could sink through the floor.

"Enough, Seth," Josh warned. "Whatever you saw, whatever you *think* you saw, is between Stacie and me. Not you. Not anyone else. Understand?"

"Absolutely," Seth said immediately.

"We're clear then."

"I saw nothing."

Josh blew out a hard breath. "Okay."

Seth's gaze shifted to the plate of eggs and his

expression brightened. "Do you mind if I grab some breakfast? I'm starved."

Stacie coasted down the street and shifted Josh's truck into Park in front of Anna's house, the scene eerily reminiscent of high school. Back then she'd feared her parents would be waiting up to give her a lecture. Now it was the thought of seeing her roommates that filled her with dread. If they were back in Denver, a sleepover would be no big deal. But here, everything felt different.

Easing the truck's door open, Stacie stepped from the vehicle and closed the door, being careful not to slam it. She cast an assessing look at the place she temporarily called home. Though the rooms upstairs were dark, lights shone in the kitchen.

That meant one, if not both, of her roommates had already started the day. It also meant if she entered through the back, she'd be asked all sorts of questions. Questions she wasn't sure she was ready to answer.

She glanced longingly at the front door, but in her heart she knew that would only postpone the inevitable. Squaring her shoulders, she followed the sidewalk to the rear of the house and pushed open the screen door.

"I'm home," she called out in a cheery tone.

"Perfect timing." Anna turned from the stove, a large wooden spoon in hand. "The oatmeal is almost ready."

While Stacie was dressed in yesterday's clothes, Anna had on a raspberry-and-cream-colored summer dress with matching sandals. Lauren was more casual. Like Stacie, the psychologist wore jeans and a cotton shirt. But Lauren's shirt was crisp and freshly ironed, not rumpled from a night on the floor.

"You're making breakfast?" Stacie couldn't keep the surprise from her voice. Though Anna was a good cook, she normally stayed out of the kitchen.

"Anna has gone domestic." Lauren glanced up from the *New York Times,* a wry smile on her lips. "I'm not sure what to make of it, but if it means a hot breakfast, I'm all for it."

"I was in the mood for oatmeal," Anna said, "and you weren't around."

"Because she spent the night with Josh." Lauren raised a coffee cup to her lips, but didn't take a drink. Instead she peered at Stacie over the rim, curiosity lighting her eyes. "How was he, by the way?"

"Lauren!" The words shot from Anna's mouth before Stacie could respond. "You don't ask about a man's sexual prowess. At least not right away."

Lauren choked on her coffee, but quickly brought herself under control. "I was asking how he was doing, not how he was in bed. Although, if someone wanted to share…"

"Josh is busy." Stacie moved to the cabinet, took out a cup and poured herself some coffee. Though she normally added cream and sugar, this time she left it black. "He and Seth and some other guys are taking the cattle to another part of his land today."

Stacie didn't quite understand the purpose of the cattle move, but she knew it was an all-day event. That's why she'd volunteered to drive herself home.

And if talking about bovines meant she didn't have to discuss her sex life, she'd chatter about the brown-and-whites all day.

"Cows remind me of dogs," Stacie said. "When they look at you with their big brown eyes, it's almost as if they can read your mind."

"You sound like Dani." Anna shook her head, but a smile lifted her lips. "Lauren and I had dinner with Seth and her at the Coffee Pot last night. She's getting so old. I can't believe she'll be seven soon."

Though Anna hadn't been keen on returning to Sweet River—even for the summer—she seemed to be enjoying the opportunity to reconnect with her family. Every time she talked about her brother and his young daughter, her eyes sparkled.

If only Paul and I could be so close, Stacie thought wistfully. But then, Seth accepted and supported Anna's dream of owning her own clothing boutique, so there was no tension between brother and sister.

Stacie fought a pang of envy.

"Seth is planning a big party for Dani," Lauren added. "We'll be invited."

From cattle drive to birthday party. Could this conversation get any crazier?

"There was a write-up in the Denver paper yesterday you should read," Anna said, changing the subject once again. "About a cooking contest."

"Who's sponsoring the contest?" Stacie asked, her interest piqued.

"Remember Jivebread? That catering firm in Denver that's so popular?" Anna asked.

"Of course." Stacie's heart skipped a beat. The firm, known for innovative recipes and eclectic cuisine, was her dream company. She'd interviewed with them a couple times, but both times lost out to more experienced chefs.

"They're looking for innovative recipes," Anna continued. "The winner gets five thousand dollars and the chance to work with their catering team for one year."

"That would be a great opportunity." Stacie kept her tone casual. "Who's doing the judging?"

Anna leaned back and grabbed a newspaper clipping from the counter. She took a sip of coffee and glanced down. "Abbie and Marc Tolliver."

Stacie groaned. Anyone else and she might have stood a chance. But with those two she was dead in the water.

Lauren glanced up from her coffee. "Is that a problem?"

"Big problem." While Stacie didn't want to be negative, she had to be realistic. "I entered a recipe in the Best of Denver competition a couple years back. Marc and Abbie were the final-round judges. They didn't like my entry at all."

While their criticism of the dish had some validity, and she'd learned from their comments, her recipe style hadn't changed much since then.

"That doesn't mean they won't like the one you submit this time," Anna said with a touching loyalty.

"Perhaps Stacie's passion has changed." Lauren took a sip of coffee and cast Stacie a pointed glance.

"From recipes to men. Or more specifically, to one certain cowboy."

"My passion hasn't changed," Stacie said firmly, her gaze shifting from one roommate to the other. "Working for Jivebread would be a dream come true. Whatever is happening between Josh and me…well, it isn't anything permanent. If I got that job I'd be outta here in a heartbeat."

Anna opened her mouth for a brief second, but instead of responding, she busied herself filling the bowls with oatmeal and placing them on the table.

"Seth mentioned he was helping Josh today." Lauren tilted her head. "Did he see you before you left?"

Oh, he'd seen her all right. Stacie didn't need to close her eyes to remember Seth's startled expression.

"Our paths crossed," Stacie drawled. "I think he was as surprised to see me as I was to see him."

"So, he knows you spent the night," Lauren said.

Stacie laughed, though right now she was finding it hard to see the humor in the situation. "Let's just say I have no doubt he knows exactly what's going on between Josh and me."

Anna dropped into the seat opposite Stacie. "What *is* going on between you and Josh?"

"Chemistry, Anna, chemistry," Lauren interjected before Stacie could answer. "Mixed with common values, it's a potent combination."

"Yeah, but I thought Stacie didn't like cowboys," Anna said, her eyes clearly puzzled.

"I didn't," Stacie said, starting to understand how a trapped animal felt, "I mean, I don't."

Lauren lifted a perfectly tweezed brow. "You don't like him, yet you slept with him?"

"I don't like the lifestyle," Stacie clarified. "But I like Josh."

"You know he was married before." Anna's expression gave nothing away.

Stacie focused her attention on sprinkling raisins over her oatmeal. "He told me."

Anna pushed her bowl aside and leaned forward, resting her forearms on the table. "Did he tell you Kristin was a city girl who made it clear to everyone in this town that being with Josh wasn't enough of a reason to stay? He didn't go out socially—even with the guys—for almost a year after she left."

There was a warning in Anna's tone that came through loud and clear. But it was the censure that raised Stacie's hackles.

"Say what you mean, Anna." Stacie held on to her rising temper with both hands.

"I don't want to see him hurt, Stace," Anna said, her eyes filled with concern. "I know he's hot. And a person would have to be blind not to see the sparks that fly whenever you're together. But he's also vulnerable."

And I'm not?

"I like him," Stacie said. "And he likes me."

Lauren added an extra dollop of brown sugar to her cereal. "Would you consider staying in Sweet River?"

"No," Stacie said. "But that's no secret. Josh knows I have to complete myself before I can be a partner to any man."

"Complete yourself?" Anna laughed. "Honey, you've been spending way too much time with Lauren."

"What she's saying makes sense," Lauren said before Stacie could respond. "There would be more happy people in this world if women and men gave themselves permission to pursue their dreams."

"Thank you, Lauren," Stacie said.

"Hey, I'm not saying Stacie should give up her dream." Anna sounded affronted that they'd even suggest such a thing. "I've just seen the way she looks at Josh."

"Don't forget the way he looks at her," Lauren added.

"Can't deny it," Stacie admitted. "There is that attraction. But it's purely sexual. And that's the way we both like it."

Chapter Eleven

Josh stood in front of Anna's house the following morning. Moving the cattle yesterday had taken until sundown. By the time he'd gotten back to the house, all he'd wanted to do was collapse into bed and sleep.

His lips curved up in a smile. He might have been dead in the saddle yesterday, but the night he'd spent with Stacie had definitely been worth it.

Josh had never been with a woman with such a capacity for giving and receiving pleasure.

Though he and Stacie had known each other only a short time, a bond of trust had formed between them. A trust that had allowed them to explore each other's bodies with boldness and passion not normally seen so early in a relationship. He hoped she didn't have any regrets. He sure didn't.

He yawned and glanced at his truck. He'd risen early and had one of his ranch hands drop him off in town. With an extra set of truck keys in his pocket, he could pick up his 4x4 and head home without disturbing anyone.

The trouble was he didn't want to jump in the truck and leave. He wanted to see Stacie. Wanted to talk to her. Most of all he wanted to make sure she was cool with what had happened. Once Seth had arrived, it had been impossible for them to talk privately.

He stared at the house. Was it only wishful thinking, or was there a light on in the back? Josh moved to the curb when the front door opened. The woman who'd taken hold of his dreams stepped onto the porch, her arms filled with four large white boxes.

Her attention was focused on closing the door, a tricky maneuver with her hands occupied elsewhere.

Josh started up the sidewalk. He increased his pace when the boxes started to tip. He sprinted up the steps when the top two slipped from her arms.

As a former wide receiver for the Sweet River Rockets, Josh had caught the winning toss in the state championship game his senior year. That experience served him well today as he stretched out his hands and pulled the boxes into his arms.

"Touchdown…Collins," the announcer's voice in his head called out.

"Josh." Stacie's voice jerked him back to the

present and stopped the victory dance before it could begin. "What are you doing here?"

Her voice was shaky and slightly breathless.

"I came to pick up the truck," he said, feeling out of breath himself. His gaze dropped to the boxes in his arms. "And to carry these."

She returned his smile and he felt himself relax. Why had he worried that seeing her again might be awkward? This was Stacie, a woman he liked...a lot.

"I'm sorry you had to come all this way for your truck," she said.

"I'm not," he said, thinking how beautiful she looked in the early-morning light. "It gave me a chance to see you again."

A hint of pink colored her cheeks. "Yes, well..."

"Where you headed?"

"The Coffee Pot," she said. "Merna buys cinnamon rolls from me Tuesday through Saturday."

He heard the satisfaction in her voice, but forced himself not to read too much into it. Stacie had made it clear she'd be leaving Sweet River by the end of the summer to search for her bliss. "I didn't know you worked for Merna."

"There's a lot about me you don't know," she said with a little laugh. "Now if I could have my boxes back, I need to scoot. Merna insists the rolls be in her hands by seven."

"I'll give you a lift." Josh gestured to his 4x4. "And I'll carry these in for you. Maybe even buy you a cup of coffee."

Stacie hesitated and for a second Josh thought

she might turn him down. Then she flashed a brilliant smile and sashayed past him, heading straight for his truck.

Stacie knew something was different the moment she opened the front door of the Coffee Pot Café. For six-fifty on a Tuesday morning, the place was hopping. Normally at this time there were only a couple grandpa types sitting by the window playing checkers. Today, the tables were occupied by card-playing retirees of both sexes.

Merna hurried to greet them, coffeepot in hand. "Thank goodness you're here. Everyone's been asking for cinnamon rolls."

Stacie felt a warm flush of pleasure. The whole-wheat sourdough rolls had been a big hit. She was sure that was why Merna had asked her to start making some specialty breads and muffins on a trial basis.

Helping out at the Coffee Pot had turned out to be a great job. Not only did she get to practice new recipes, but she got a paycheck for doing what she loved.

"What's with the crowd?" Stacie asked as Josh placed the boxes on the counter.

"Pitch tournament," Merna said. "Started at six-thirty."

"So early?" Stacie couldn't hide her surprise. She'd always thought people retired so they could sleep late.

"Everyone here has gotten up before dawn most

of their lives." Merna's tone reflected genuine fondness for her customers. "In fact, they were crowded around the door when I arrived at six."

"Anticipating Stacie's fabulous cinnamon rolls, no doubt." Josh shot her a wink.

"The rolls—oh my goodness—we need to get them on plates immediately." Merna turned to the woman coming out of the kitchen. "Shirley, could you help me get these dished up?"

"I'll help, too," Stacie said.

Merna shook her head. "You did your part making them."

"It was no trouble." Stacie glanced at Josh and smiled. "I love to bake."

"Yes, but because of the rolls, you and Josh had to get up early. I remember what it was like when my Harold was alive. Mornings were our best time to cuddle."

For a moment, the words hung in the air. Stacie willed her cheeks not to warm.

"Josh didn't spend the night, Merna." Stacie kept her tone even, being careful not to protest too much and give credence to Merna's comment. As far as anyone knew, she and Josh were just casual acquaintances. That's how she wanted it to stay.

Josh was already known around town as the cowboy one city girl had left in the dust. Stacie refused to make it two.

Josh bided his time while he parked the truck in Anna's driveway. Stacie had been different on the drive back, more reserved and determined to keep the conversation general.

He first noticed the change in her demeanor when Merna had made the comment about them sleeping together. Josh didn't like the fact people were gossiping, but this was a small town and it came with the territory. There wasn't anything he could do to stop it.

"Thanks for the ride," Stacie said in that pleasant voice women used when giving a guy the brush-off. "I'd better go."

She reached for the door handle and stepped out, not even giving him a chance to open it for her.

He jumped out and caught her on her way around the truck. The bare skin of her arm was warm beneath his fingers.

She paused and the look of longing in her eyes gave him hope that he still had a shot.

"Will you go with me to a baseball game Saturday night?" Josh couldn't remember the last time he'd felt so unsure of himself, but he pressed forward despite his unease. "Sweet River is playing Big Timber. Should be a good game."

He thought he saw a spark of interest at the mention of baseball, but it fled so quickly he decided he'd been mistaken.

"Thanks for the invitation." She played with her watch, twisting it back and forth. "But I don't think it's a good idea."

He felt as if he'd taken a sucker punch to the gut. But he warned himself not to jump to conclusions.

What wasn't a good idea? The baseball game? The day of the week? Or dating him?

"Is it me?" Somehow he managed to keep a smile on his face. "Or don't you like baseball?"

She hesitated and he knew she was dumping him.

"We decided our first time together that dating wasn't a good idea," Stacie said.

"We did." Josh wasn't sure what had brought about her abrupt change of heart. And what about her offer of a fling? Was she taking that back, too?

The look in her eyes gave him that answer. If she wanted to change her mind, that was her prerogative. But that didn't mean he understood.

As he walked her to the front porch, he found himself talking about the dry spell the area had been experiencing. They'd discussed the weather on this porch the first time they'd been together. It only seemed fitting they'd discuss it on the last.

"I don't understand why you didn't go with Josh when you had the chance," Anna said. "The guy is a baseball fanatic."

Stacie walked beside Anna down the sidewalk, wishing her friend would drop the subject. In the past four days they'd had this discussion more times than she could count. "He's out of town this weekend...remember?"

"But he wouldn't be in Billings today if you'd agreed to go with him," Anna pointed out. "He would have waited until next Thursday, when he'd already be in town for the cattle auction."

"I didn't have a choice." Stacie heaved an exasperated breath. "Our relationship was starting to become front-page news in this town. I didn't want people talking, especially when I left, saying he couldn't satisfy me just like he hadn't been able to satisfy Kristin."

"But—"

"You told me not to hurt him," Stacie reminded her friend. "That's what I'm trying not to do."

Anna's gaze grew thoughtful. "Did Josh say the gossip bothered him? Or that he didn't want to date you anymore?"

Stacie gritted her teeth and counted to ten. "No. It was my decision."

"Because you were afraid he'd break up with you?"

"Oh, for goodness sakes, Anna, drop it." Couldn't her friend see she was just trying to do what was best for Josh? If she didn't care, she'd ignore the fact that somebody was going to get hurt. "Let's talk about something else. Tell me about Sweet River's baseball team."

From the time she'd been old enough to pick up a Wiffle ball, Stacie had loved America's favorite pastime. Though she hadn't been blessed with the natural talent for sports like her siblings, she'd always been a passionate spectator.

"The team is coed, which is cool," Anna said, going along with the change in topic. "It's made up of former high school and college players from the area. The town really gets behind them. Tonight they're playing their rival, Big Timber."

That told Stacie the stadium would be packed. The realization reinforced that she'd been right to turn down Josh's offer. Although, she thought wistfully, going with him would have been fun. Anna had little interest in the sport. Still, when Stacie had mentioned that she'd like to attend the game, Anna had good-naturedly agreed to go with her.

The closer they got to the ball field, the more people they saw. Even after years away, Anna knew almost everyone. And Stacie discovered she had her own fan club.

"I swear," Anna said, after another person stopped them, "your cinnamon rolls might be the hottest things ever to hit this town!"

Stacie had spent so many years with little reinforcement of her cooking skills, she loved the compliments. "I'm happy people like what I make. And I'm so grateful to Merna for giving me the opportunity to do what I love. Sweet River is lucky to have such a nice café."

"I sure hope that continues," Anna said cryptically.

"What are you talking about?"

"Rumor is Merna may sell and move back to California."

"She hasn't mentioned that to me." Though Stacie wouldn't be around to see the place sold, she found the news distressing. She knew what the café meant to the community. It wasn't just a place to eat, but a place for citizens to congregate and connect.

"Maybe Shirley will take over." Stacie thought aloud. "She runs the place when Merna's away."

"She'd be the logical successor," Anna agreed. "But maybe she doesn't have the money. Or doesn't want to shoulder all the responsibility."

"Is that why Merna's selling?" Stacie asked. "Because she needs money?"

"I heard Merna's daughter in California is going through a divorce and wants her mom with her."

"I can't believe she hasn't said anything to me."

"It may not happen," Anna said, seemingly unconcerned. "It's not like people are busting down the doors to buy businesses in Sweet River."

"I guess—"

"Don't worry. I'm sure it'll be at least another couple months," Anna said. "You'll have a job until you're ready to leave."

Stacie realized that Anna had misinterpreted her concern. She didn't care about herself. She worried what was going to happen to Al and Norm, who played checkers there every morning. And to the ladies who came in on Thursday for lunch and stayed to play bridge. Not to mention, where would the kids who stopped in after school go?

"Nice evening for a ball game."

Stacie turned. It took her a second to recognize Pastor Barbee. Wearing a blue T-shirt and ball cap, he bore little resemblance to the minister who preached from the pulpit every Sunday. His wife had also gone ultracasual in a powder-blue jumpsuit.

"I thought you'd be here with Joshua." Mrs.

Barbee glanced around as if expecting the cowboy to magically appear.

Stacie gestured to her friend. "I'm here with Anna."

Anna smiled, lifting a hand and wiggling her fingers.

"You two girls stay out of trouble," Pastor Barbee said in a hearty voice.

"Good luck finding Joshua," Mrs. Barbee called out as she and Anna continued down the sidewalk.

Anna grinned. "Small-town living at its best."

The two laughed and continued toward the ball field. With each step Stacie's excitement grew. "I can't believe Lauren didn't want to come."

"I don't think Lauren has ever been to a baseball game." Anna chuckled. "Not her childhood activity. Too lowbrow for her father."

From the little Lauren said about her dad, Anna was probably right in her assessment. The couple of times Stacie had met the respected researcher and university professor, he'd been polite, but a bit scary in his intensity. Definitely not the kind of guy she'd picture with hot dogs and beer at a baseball game.

"Maybe one day she'll give it a try." Stacie looped her arm through Anna's and gave it a quick squeeze. "I'm glad you came with me."

"There it is," Anna said when they turned a corner.

A wave of nostalgia washed over Stacie. The ballpark reminded Stacie of her high school baseball stadium with the sections of wooden bleachers flanking home plate. Only these bleacher seats were painted a bright robin's-egg blue.

Anna tugged on her arm. "Let's get some food."

They'd barely eaten their kraut dogs when Anna started complaining that her stomach hurt. After two urgent trips to the restrooms Anna found an old friend to give her a lift home.

Stacie had been determined to see her sick room-mate safely home, but her friend wouldn't hear of it. So before the first pitch had even been thrown, Stacie found herself sitting at the top of the stands... alone.

She took a sip of ice-cold beer and glanced around the stands, amazed at the number of people she recognized. She'd just finished checking out the Sweet River bench when she saw Josh.

Her breath caught in her throat. What was *he* doing here? Though Stacie told herself to look away, her gaze remained riveted on him. He didn't see her, so she took her time looking. He was standing at the end of a bleacher talking to an older gentleman.

Like many Sweet River fans, Josh wore a blue shirt in support of the local team. The fabric accentuated the obvious width of his shoulders. She couldn't help remembering how the muscles in his back had flexed when she'd caressed him.

She swallowed hard against the sudden ache in her chest. Not seeing him, not talking to him, had made the past four days unbearable. But keeping her distance was necessary. If they'd stayed together any longer, they'd be considered a couple. Expectations by the locals would rise only to be dashed when she left town. She would not have the town laughing at Josh or gossiping about his inability to satisfy a big-city girl.

Still, what would it hurt to be polite and say hello? She'd half risen from her seat when she caught sight of Wes Danker returning from the concession stand with two pretty girls close behind. One of the young women had a mass of dark, curly hair and a bright smile. The other was a well-endowed blonde.

Misty.

Stacie sank down, bile rising to her throat. Had Josh called the blonde when she'd turned down his date? Was that why he'd returned early from Billings? Was Misty Josh's new fling?

A twinge of something that felt an awful lot like jealousy stabbed Stacie's heart. The kraut dog— Anna's nemesis—turned to a leaden weight in her stomach.

Wes gestured to the empty seats and Josh stepped aside to let the three pass. Stacie noticed Misty went last, ensuring she would be sitting by Josh.

"Is that seat taken?"

Stacie pulled her gaze from Josh to find Alexander Darst standing in the aisle. Instead of wearing shorts or jeans and a T-shirt like most of the spectators, her first "match" wore dress pants and a shirt open at the collar. The attorney's only concession to the informal event seemed to be leaving his tie at home.

Stacie smiled. "It's available."

"I wasn't sure I'd make the opening pitch." Alex

maneuvered past her and sat down. "I got caught up with some work at the office."

"Today's Saturday."

Alex shrugged. "Only time the client could make it."

Stacie didn't know why she was surprised. Her brother worked weekends. Back in Denver, many of her high-achieving friends routinely put in sixty-plus-hour weeks. But Stacie realized one of the things she loved about Sweet River was its slower pace. Oddly enough, the kind of place that used to drive her crazy had become her new gold standard. Who'd have guessed?

"Do you like baseball?" she asked Alex.

"Not particularly." He settled next to her. "But every person in these stands is a potential client. I decided it was time to get out and mingle. What about you?"

"I came with my friend Anna," Stacie said. "She wasn't feeling well and had to leave. I love baseball so I stayed."

"Lucky for me." He flashed a smile.

Stacie wondered how she could have ever thought he was good-looking. Though his hair had obviously been cut by a stylist and his dress pants were hand tailored, his features were too perfect, his body a little too lean.

He also had an annoying habit of talking continuously. She listened to him ramble through eight innings, sneaking a peek now and then at Misty and Josh. But when Misty leaned her head against Josh's shoulder, Stacie had seen enough.

She pressed her lips together and pulled a sheet of paper and a pen from her purse. Although the game was nearly over, she started recording strikes, balls and errors.

"What are you doing?" Alex asked.

"Keeping stats," she said between clenched teeth, resisting the urge to glance down at Josh and Misty. "My brothers played ball and my father used to keep the books for the coaches. He taught me how to do it."

"Sounds like you and your dad are close."

She could hear the envy in his voice, and with a start she realized it was true. She and her father *had* been close. Until he'd decided to try to ruin—er, run—her life. "We were…I mean, we are close."

"You're lucky," he said. "My father had expectations I could never seem to meet."

Something in his tone caused Stacie to really look at Alex. The sadness lurking in his eyes surprised her. "I bet he's proud of you now."

"He wanted me to go into corporate law," Alex said. "I wanted to live in a small town and do a little bit of everything."

"How did you end up here?" She couldn't remember if he'd told her on their "date."

"We came to Montana on vacation when I was a small boy. I loved the mountains and the wide-open spaces in between. When I got out of law school, I tried it his way. I practiced in Chicago until I moved here."

"How do you like being a Sweet River resident?" She waited for him to start raving.

"A little disappointing," he said instead.

"How so?" Stacie asked.

"The people in this area are cautious." He paused and appeared to choose his words carefully. "Many of them choose to make the trip to Big Timber for their legal needs rather than come to a stranger."

Stacie pulled her brows together. She understood what he was saying, but it didn't make sense. "I've been here less time than you, but I've found everyone to be more than welcoming."

"That's probably because one of your friends is from here," Alex pointed out. "And aren't you dating a local?"

"He and I were—we are—just friends." Stacie didn't elaborate. Talking to this man about Josh didn't feel right. "Are you thinking of moving back to Chicago?"

"No," Alex said, then more firmly as if trying to convince himself: "No. I'm sure, given time, business will improve."

Alex seemed sincere and Stacie found herself wanting to help him. "Have you ever thought of maybe…I don't know…dressing more…casually?"

She softened the suggestion with a smile.

"Wear jeans and a T-shirt to the office?" Alex shuddered. "I couldn't. It wouldn't be professional."

"I'm not talking about the office," Stacie said. "I'm talking about now, at a sporting event. You don't wear dress pants and Italian leather shoes to a ball game, not if you want to fit in."

"I suppose—"

"And another thing, the Clipper is a barbershop on Main Street, a block from the Coffee Pot Café. Give them a try. If you patronize local merchants, maybe they'll support your business."

She half expected Alex to scoff at her suggestions. Instead he appeared to be seriously considering them.

"You like it here," he said at last.

"What?"

"You like it here…in Sweet River."

"Of course," she said. "It's a great place."

"Have you decided to stay?" His gaze was curious. "I know when we went out you couldn't wait to get back to Denver, but you seem more settled now."

"I've—"

The crack of a bat split the air and Stacie and Alex rose to their feet along with the rest of the crowd. It was bottom of the ninth, Sweet River at bat and trailing by one run. With a runner on base, this was her team's chance to bring home a victory.

"Go. Go!" Stacie yelled.

The runners rounded the bases. When the batter slid into home plate, the crowd roared and Stacie jumped up and down, hugging everyone in sight. When Alex hugged her, she hugged him back. Joy sluiced through her. She was on top of the world until her gaze dropped to the field and she saw Josh staring up at her, a look of stunned disbelief on his face.

Chapter Twelve

Josh's heart stopped beating then started up with a sputter. Now he understood why Stacie had dumped him. It made sense she'd pick a guy who looked like he'd stepped off the cover of *GQ* rather than a cowboy with dirt on his boots.

The first time they'd met she'd made it clear she didn't like cowboys. But he thought she'd changed her mind. *Obviously not.* He clenched his teeth.

"Hey, Collins." Wes poked him in the ribs. "We're going to Earl's to celebrate the V."

Josh shifted his gaze to Wes and the two women. He'd gotten back early from Billings and had called his friend to see if he was going to the game. Wes hadn't mentioned anything about bringing Sasha and Misty along.

Though Misty seemed like a nice person, she wasn't his type, and the last thing Josh wanted was to prolong the evening. But the pleading look in Wes's eyes stopped the refusal pushing against his lips. Something told him if he said no, the girls might go their own way. It didn't matter to him, but he knew it mattered to Wes.

"I'll go," Josh said. "For a little while."

"It's karaoke night." Misty slipped her arm though his. "Wait until you hear me sing. I'm really good."

Josh's first impulse was to pull back from the possessive gesture. But he sensed Stacie watching him, so he smiled at the buxom blonde instead. "Tell me more about yourself. We didn't get a chance to talk much during the game."

Actually there had been ample time, but he'd been too busy brooding about Stacie to pay Misty much attention. The blonde was a country girl. That much he remembered from Wes's brief introduction. Grew up on a ranch close to Cheyenne.

"Did I tell you me and Sasha filled out one of those surveys for that professor lady?" Misty tightened her hold on him, forcing her breast against his arm. "We have so much in common, what with us both being country folk. I bet they match me with you."

Josh didn't know what to say. Misty was right. She should have been the perfect woman for him. There was only one problem—she wasn't Stacie.

Misty chattered happily on the way to Earl's Tavern, a cowboy bar around the corner from the

Coffee Pot Café. Wes found a parking spot not far from where Josh had left his truck.

As he walked past the café, Josh couldn't help remembering how good things had been between him and Stacie just four days ago. Until that morning he'd helped her deliver—

"I love their cinnamon rolls," Misty said, interrupting her story about her barrel-racing days. "Sasha and me come here on our day off just to get one of those rolls."

"They're humongous," Sasha added. "And super yummy."

Wes cast a pointed glance at Josh as if waiting for him to comment. But as far as Josh was concerned the less said about those damned cinnamon rolls, the better.

"Josh knows the woman who makes 'em," Wes said. "She—"

The big man was picking up steam and would have said more, but Josh shot him a quelling glance. The last thing he wanted to talk about, to think about tonight, was Stacie Summers.

"Anyway," Wes said, quickly switching gears, "I like 'em, too." He patted his belly. "Some might say I like them a little too much."

The girls giggled.

For a moment, blessed silence descended. Until Misty started talking about the time she'd made it to the semifinals on the national rodeo circuit.

By the time they reached the tavern, Josh was ready to bolt. Wes must have sensed it because he motioned to a large round table toward the back of the bar.

"Why don't you three grab that one so we're sure to have a seat," Wes said. "I'll order the pizza and beer."

"We have to sign up for karaoke." Misty slanted a sideways glance at Josh. "Everyone says I sound like Shania."

Josh forced a weak smile. Once they were out of earshot he turned to Wes. "She's driving me crazy. I've got to—"

"Tune her out," Wes said. "Just give me fifteen minutes. That's all I'm asking."

Josh glanced longingly at the door.

"Then, if you want, you can leave," Wes said. "I won't try to stop you."

"I'll give you fifteen minutes, Wes," Josh warned. "Then I'm outta here."

Josh headed to the back table. Wes was right about one thing: the place was filling up quickly. After only a few minutes, every table was taken and Misty had moved on to how she'd gotten her job at the dude ranch.

Josh listened politely, but his thoughts kept returning to the town's new attorney.

Misty paused in her story just long enough to take a breath and Josh realized one of the things he'd really liked about Stacie was that she wasn't in love with hearing herself talk.

Wes arrived before Misty took another breath, but he wasn't alone. "Guess who I found looking for a table? I told them they could join us."

Even before Josh looked up, the scent of jasmine told him who he'd find standing there. It took everything he had to force a smile to his lips and resist the urge to throttle Wes.

Josh stood and extended his hand to the man. "Josh Collins," he said by way of introduction. "I have a ranch about forty miles from here."

The man returned Josh's strained smile with a friendly one of his own. "Alexander Darst. I'm the new attorney in town."

"Good to finally meet you." The first thing Josh noticed was the lack of calluses on the man's hands. The second was his size. The guy was on the smaller side—built the way Stacie had once told him she liked her men. His heart twisted.

"Nice to see you again, Josh," Stacie said in a soft voice that sounded lyrical next to Misty's nasally whine.

Josh shifted his gaze, surprised at the absence of her usual heart-stopping smile. Until he reminded himself that her happiness wasn't his concern. Not anymore. Not since she'd kicked him out of her life and taken up with a city dude.

He settled for giving her a nod of acknowledgment. But old habits died hard, and when she rounded the table to take the open seat next to him, he found himself pulling out her chair.

"Thanks," she said.

When her gaze met his, he looked away, afraid of what his eyes might reveal.

Thankfully the pizza came, along with a pitcher of beer and a couple of extra glasses for Alex and Stacie.

Alex hesitated. "I wonder if they serve wine—"

Josh wasn't sure what the glance Stacie sent the attorney meant, but Alex shut his mouth, grabbed the pitcher and filled Stacie's glass and his own.

Though the fifteen minutes Josh had given Wes were up, there was no way he could leave now. Not without it looking like he was running from Stacie. So he tried to keep his attention on the conversation and off her. It wasn't easy. When she was near, his body operated on a heightened state of awareness.

"On deck, Misty and Sasha," the DJ called out.

Misty squealed and jumped up, jerking Sasha to her feet. "Wish us luck."

"Good luck," Josh said, relieved when the two headed to the stage.

It didn't take more than a couple seconds for him to realize he had a problem. While he was happy that Misty was gone, when she'd been at the table he could focus all his attention on her. Now Wes and Alex were talking investment strategies, leaving him no choice but to make conversation with Stacie.

"What did you think of the game?" Stacie's smile was hesitant, and for the first time Josh realized this was as awkward for her as it was for him.

"It was good." Josh turned in his seat to face her. "What did you think?"

"The come-from-behind ending was super exciting." Her fingers tightened around her glass of beer.

"I was jumping up and down and hugging everyone in sight."

The words hung in the air. Josh stilled. Was this her way of telling him there was nothing between her and the attorney? But if that were true, why had she gone to the game with him in the first place?

You're reading too much into a simple comment. He's the type of guy she's been looking for, not you, he told himself.

"I was surprised to see you with Darst." Josh forced his expression to remain neutral, his tone off-hand, as if he were talking cattle prices with another rancher. "When did you two start dating?"

"Dating?" Stacie made a face. "I'm not dating Alex. He's a nice guy, but not for me."

Josh's heart did a series of flip-flops. He cleared his throat. "You were at the game with him. You're with him now."

"Are you and Misty on a date?"

"No. Absolutely not."

"You were at the game with her," Stacie pointed out. "You're with her now."

"Wes brought her along." Josh wondered when he'd been switched from offense to defense. "I came with them to get a beer, but Misty and I are definitely not together."

"I went to the game with Anna," Stacie explained, her tone as matter-of-fact as his. "But she got sick and went home. Alex came late and happened to sit beside me."

"You hugged him," Josh said.

"I hugged everyone around me. I was happy we won." Stacie met his gaze. "But I didn't hug any of those people like I hug you. I don't hug anyone that way."

Though the bar was dimly lit, there was no mistaking the emotion in her eyes. Josh found himself more confused than ever.

"You dumped me," Josh said. "Everything was great between us. Then, all of a sudden, you decide you didn't want to see me again."

"That's not how it was," she said, glancing at Alex and Wes, as if making sure they weren't listening.

"That's how it felt." It was as close as Josh could come to baring his soul.

The women finished their karaoke rendition of "That Don't Impress Me Much" and the room erupted into applause. Josh put his hands together and clapped with the others. Misty was right about one thing. She *could* sing.

Still, he groaned when they started back to the table. His groan turned to a silent cheer when Misty and Sasha stopped to flirt with a group of rowdy, admiring cowboys.

"We need to talk," Stacie said. "But not here."

Though Misty was occupied for the moment, Josh knew it would be more difficult to get away once she came back. He hadn't asked Misty on a date, so as far as he was concerned he was a free agent. But Stacie, on the other hand...

"What about Alex?"

Stacie lifted her chin. "I already answered that question."

Josh knew the clock was running out. He could hold on to his pride and tell Stacie there was nothing to discuss. But he still had questions. And she was the only one with the answers.

He rose to his feet and Stacie stood, as well. When Wes and Alex paused mid-conversation, Josh reached into his pocket, pulled out a couple of bills and tossed them on the table.

"I'm taking Stacie home," Josh said, keeping his tone casual.

Wes's gaze turned speculative. "I guess I'll see you later."

Josh nodded and turned his attention briefly to the attorney. "Good to meet you, Darst."

Alex's gaze shifted from Stacie to Josh. "Likewise."

When Josh walked out of Earl's Tavern, it was with a lighter step than when he'd entered. Stacie was at his side and he was taking her home.

The only question that remained was would they end up at her house? Or his?

Stacie had hoped that she and Josh could sit on one of the metal benches scattered on Sweet River's Main Street. But too many people still mingled on the sidewalks to make a private conversation possible.

She could take him back to Anna's house, but they'd face the same problem there. Because her reason for breaking up with Josh centered on her

concern for his reputation, being seen together—
even if they were just talking—wasn't a good idea.

"Could we go for a drive?" Stacie asked. "I know
gas is expensive but—"

"My truck is parked around the corner." His expression gave nothing away.

Stacie hurried to the vehicle. Not until she was
safely in the cab and they were on a road headed out
of town did she relax. She cast Josh a sideways
glance. "You have questions."

"A few."

Okay, so he wasn't going to make this easy. In a
way she didn't blame him. The past four days had
been hard on her, but she'd at least known why it was
best they remain apart. He hadn't a clue.

And that was *her* fault.

Shame rose inside her. When Merna had made her
speculative comment, it had been a wake-up call.
People could end up hurt—*Josh* could end up hurt—
by their fling.

"I probably seem like a flake." She gave a humor-
less laugh. "Hot to cold in sixty seconds."

"I don't understand what's going on in your
head," he said in a low voice. "That's why I'm here.
So I can understand."

"It's because of you," Stacie blurted out, her heart
aching at the hurt and confusion in his voice and
knowing it was all because of her. "I did it because
of you."

His fingers tightened around the steering wheel
and a tiny muscle in his jaw jumped. "Is it because

I'm a cowboy? Because I'm not the kind of man you want...even for a fling?"

"No." Stacie blinked back tears, realizing just how much her actions had hurt him. "It was because I didn't want to see you hurt. I don't want people talking about you after I'm gone, calling you the man city girls always leave. Don't you understand? I couldn't bear that."

Several stray tears slipped down her cheeks. She quickly brushed them aside, hoping he hadn't noticed.

"Are you telling me this is all about *gossip?*" His voice grew louder with each word.

"I don't want anyone to laugh at you." Stacie's heart rose to her throat and shattered in two. "Not ever. And certainly not because of me."

"You don't want to hurt me." It came out as a statement rather than a question.

"Never."

"Then take back your goodbye." The muscle in his jaw jumped. "I can deal with gossip."

"When I leave, it's going to be hard." Stacie couldn't resist anymore. She reached over and took his hand. "Painful. Really, really painful. For both of us."

When the words slipped from her tongue, she knew Anna had been right. She wasn't just worried about Josh being hurt by the gossip. She was also worried about herself. Worried that she wouldn't be able to leave him when the time came.

But she wanted—no, *needed*—to find her bliss.

"I'm willing to take that risk," he said quietly. "The question is…are you?"

Josh turned off the highway onto a country road, but Stacie paid little attention. Her head was swimming. Could she do it? Could she spend two more months with this man and then walk away?

"The baseball game would have been more fun if we'd been together," Josh said in a persuasive tone. "We enjoy each other's company. Why should we both be alone these next couple months?"

Still, Stacie hesitated. "The gossip won't bother you?"

Josh chuckled. "Do I look like the kind of guy who pays attention to that stuff?"

"No," she said, then more firmly: "No, you don't."

"Well?"

She opened her mouth, but the sound of barking dogs stopped her. Bert and her pups ran alongside the truck as it drove down a familiar lane.

"This is your place."

"Last I checked."

"Why are we here?"

"I said I was taking you home." He pulled the truck to a stop and his lips hitched up in a lazy smile. "I didn't say *whose* home."

Dear God, she adored this man. "If you're expecting me to sleep over you need to know I didn't bring any pajamas."

He grinned. "Not a problem."

A surge of emotion blinded Stacie with its intensity. She didn't just adore this man, she *loved* him. With that realization came a certainty that she was right where she wanted—and needed—to be, at least for now.

The next month felt like a dream. Sometimes Josh wanted to pinch himself to make sure it was real. He'd never been happier. He and Stacie spent every free moment together.

One day she even rode with him to look for stray calves. They'd ended up making love under the noonday sun and the bright blue sky.

Today he was meeting Stacie for lunch while in town picking up supplies. He'd already gotten what he needed from Sweet River Grain and Feed and he had thirty minutes to kill. He turned onto Main Street and parked in front of the bank. A half hour was more than enough time to accommodate a quick side trip to see his dad.

There had been a message on his answering machine last night from his father asking him to stop by the next time he was in town.

Josh waved at the teller as he headed to the back of the bank. His father's door was open and Bill Collins looked up when Josh entered the office.

A smile of welcome split his father's tanned face. "Come in, son. Shut the door so we have some privacy."

Josh found the request unusual. The last time they'd shut the door had been when Josh told his dad Kristin had left him.

"You're looking good." His father nodded approvingly. "Happier than I remember."

"Things are going well at the ranch." Josh glanced at the clock on the wall, taking note of the time.

"I've heard things are on the upswing in your personal life, too." His father motioned for him to take a seat in the leather wingback in front of the desk.

Josh dropped into the chair. He shifted, unable to get comfortable. "You could say that."

"Your mom and I would like to meet your new girlfriend," his father said. "Especially since things seem to be getting serious."

"We're not serious." Josh gave his dad the same answer he gave everyone who asked. "Stacie and I are just good friends."

"That's not what we've heard."

Josh kept his smile easy. "I'd have thought you'd lived in this town long enough to know not to listen to gossip."

"Rosalee told your mother Miss Summers frequently spends the night."

Josh's smile froze on his face. Rosalee Barker was the woman he employed to cook and clean. She'd worked for his parents for years before semiretiring. Nevertheless, she worked for him now and he thought she could be trusted to keep his privacy. "Rosalee just lost herself a job."

"Don't be angry." His dad held up both hands. "Rosalee only told your mother. You know she's not going to say anything."

"Mom told you," Josh pointed out.

"We know you wouldn't be with this woman if you didn't care for her." His father's brows pulled together. "What I don't understand is why you're being so secretive. It's not like you."

"This isn't high school, Dad." Josh kept his tone light. "You don't need to meet everyone I date."

"We like to meet the ones who are important to you," his father said smoothly. "Come over for dinner tomorrow night around six. We'll keep things nice and casual."

"Not a good idea."

"Why not?"

"I know how it'd go. You'd start asking about our future." Josh could just imagine the look on Stacie's face if his mother began talking about her desire for grandchildren. "Since we don't have a future, that would be awkward. Stacie will be leaving Sweet River before long. That will be the end of our relationship."

"You don't plan to keep in touch?"

"What would be the point?" Frustration made Josh's voice harsher than he'd intended. He'd considered that option, but he knew it would only be postponing the inevitable. "She doesn't want to live here. That's the bottom line."

"Does she know you love her?" His father rose to his feet and walked to the window.

"What makes you think I love her?"

"You're my son," his dad said, his gaze still focused outside. "I know you."

Josh wanted to deny his feelings for Stacie, but

he couldn't. "What would be the point in telling her? Stacie needs to choose her own course in life."

Bill Collins turned. "In business, you need *all* the facts to make a good decision."

His dad made it sound simple, but Josh knew how much finding her bliss meant to Stacie. Telling her he loved her would be the equivalent of emotional blackmail.

He wasn't going to do it. Not even if it meant losing the woman he loved.

Chapter Thirteen

Stacie parked the Jeep on the shoulder of the long lane leading up to Seth Anderssen's house. Obviously this was more than a child-blowing-out-candles-and-opening-gifts party.

She glanced over at Lauren. "I can see why Seth insisted on such a big cake."

"I hope I look okay." Lauren snapped the vanity mirror shut. "I didn't want to be too casual, but now I'm worried I went the other way."

Stacie didn't immediately respond. She wasn't sure what to make of Lauren's behavior. Her roommate had changed outfits five times before leaving the house and she'd been fussing with her makeup since they'd pulled out of Sweet River.

"You look amazing." While Lauren's sleeveless linen sheath was simple, the periwinkle-blue color said this professor could be fun, too. "Very professional."

Lauren's face blanched. "Professional?"

Stacie blinked. Lauren's tone made her compliment sound like a bad thing. "I thought that was the image you were trying to project."

Her roommate had been counting down the days until the party. Stacie had assumed it was because a lot of Seth's single friends would be there. While she didn't expect Lauren to actively recruit survey participants during Dani's special day, she *had* expected her to be in full businesswoman mode.

"What was I thinking?" Lauren's face fell. "I *am* overdressed."

Sensing whatever she said wouldn't be right, Stacie opted for silence. She focused on pulling the keys from the ignition and dropping them in her purse.

"Take a good look at me. I want you to be completely honest," Lauren said. "Am I overdressed?"

Reluctantly, Stacie shifted her gaze. She studied her friend with a critical eye, determined to give a fair appraisal. "The pearls *may* be a bit over the top, but then again I don't know what is de rigueur for these events. Remember, this is all new to me, too."

Like Lauren, Stacie had debated what to wear. Knowing everything in Sweet River tended to be casual, Stacie had opted for pants and a top made of gold silk and embroidered with little designs. The outfit reminded her of Chinese pajamas. Anna said the color made her hazel eyes look more amber than green.

"I must change." Lauren's voice sounded shrill in the car's silence. "I can't go in there looking like this."

For a second Stacie thought her roommate was kidding. After all, Lauren was the quintessential academic. Logic over emotion. Then Stacie took a closer look. Dear God, were those really *tears* in the beautiful blonde's eyes?

Stacie's heart twisted at Lauren's distress. Finding males for her research was obviously taking its toll on her friend. Stacie turned in the seat and offered a reassuring smile. "Why would you change? You are fantastic in that dress. The color makes your eyes look violet, and the style suits your fabulous figure."

Lauren dabbed at her eyes with a tissue. "Do you think Seth will be impressed?"

"Does it matter?"

Lauren's cheeks turned a dusty pink. "He's a handsome man. A woman likes to look her best."

Stacie paused, the puzzle pieces finally falling into place. She gave a whoop. "You have the hots for Anna's brother."

The pink dusting Lauren's cheeks darkened to a deep rose. "I do not have the 'hots' for him." Her tone was a touch indignant and classic Lauren. "But I do like him as a person. And in case you've forgotten, Seth is the number-one reason I was able to get enough subjects to complete my research."

The flush on Lauren's cheeks and the sparkle in her eyes told Stacie that her friend's feelings went beyond gratitude. But the tilt of Lauren's chin said this wasn't the time to press for deeper emotions.

"He'll think you look beautiful," Stacie said.

Lauren's stiff shoulders relaxed. She took a deep, steadying breath. After retouching her lipstick and powdering her nose, she reached for the door handle. "I'm ready now."

Thank you, Jesus.

Though they'd discussed what would happen once they got to the ranch, Lauren had been so stressed during the ride that Stacie wasn't sure if any of what she'd said had registered. "Don't forget I need help getting the cake inside."

Lauren glanced down at her spiky heels. "Why don't I carry the salad and send someone back to help you with the cake?"

"That's fine," Stacie said. "I'll wait."

When Lauren disappeared around the bend in the drive, Stacie moved to the back of the Jeep to ready the cake.

"I can carry it for you."

A warmth flowed through Stacie's veins like warm honey. She turned and there he was, standing in the gravel drive, his dark hair tousled by the breeze. Her heart did a happy dance in her chest. "Josh. I thought you were in Bozeman."

Josh smiled. "I came back early. I couldn't wait any longer to see you."

Her heart fluttered and suddenly she found herself

drowning in his eyes. She'd dated her share of men, but no one who'd touched her heart. Until this cowboy.

She'd told herself over and over the past three days that she needed to take a step back from the relationship. It wasn't good to miss someone so much.

With that in mind, she tore her gaze from his and popped the hatch. After lowering the end gate, she tugged the cardboard box toward her.

Josh moved to her side. He leaned over her shoulder, clearly curious. "What's in the box?"

"A 'Cinderella and Her Castle' cake." Several years ago Stacie had done a stint as a baker's assistant at a wedding shop in Denver. It had felt good to use those skills again. "Want to see it?"

"You know I do," he said, his warm breath tickling her ear as he planted a kiss on her neck.

A delicious shiver of wanting washed over her. But she forced herself to ignore the sensation and instead focused on lifting the top off the box.

A low whistle escaped Josh's lips. "You made that?"

"I did indeed." Stacie surveyed her masterpiece, feeling like a new mother showing off her firstborn.

He peered closer. His eyes widened. "The castle sparkles—"

"Edible food glitter."

"The turrets with the flags?"

"Sugar cones, construction paper and toothpicks."

"Wow." Admiration filled his gaze. "You are one talented lady."

Like any pretty girl, Stacie had received her share of compliments over the years. But this was different. This wasn't about looks. This was about talent.

Who'd have thought a *cowboy* would be the one to understand her so well? "Thank you, Josh."

"You *will* find your bliss." His tone left no room for doubt. "You're too creative and talented not to."

Stacie carefully replaced the lid and pulled the box closer, wondering why she didn't feel more excited at the prospect.

"How'd you end up doing the cake? Last I heard Merna was making it."

"Seth said Merna had caught that flu that was going around." Stacie struggled to remember his exact words. "He'd already tried a woman in Big Timber, but she was booked."

"You came to his rescue."

"What can I say?" Stacie said with a laugh. "I'm a nice person."

"Yes, you are." His gaze wrapped around her, holding her close. Familiar warmth washed over her.

"I've missed you," she said softly, ignoring the warning flags popping up.

Josh opened his arms. "Come here."

Stacie didn't hesitate. Josh had been out of town on some ranch business for three long days, and she'd missed him terribly.

She laid her head against his chest and listened to the beat of his heart. Strong and steady, like the man himself. Only with him did she feel safe... cherished...loved.

"You're shivering." He leaned back and held her at arm's length, his brow furrowed in worry. "Do you feel okay?"

She slid a finger down his cheek. Though she knew every inch of his body, right now she felt as if she could explore it forever. "Like I said, I missed you."

Josh captured her hand and planted a kiss in her palm, his gaze never leaving hers. "Maybe I should go away more often."

"Don't you dare."

"Come home with me tonight," he said suddenly.

Instead of answering she slipped her arms around his waist and tugged him close, inhaling the clean, fresh scent of him. "You showered with my favorite soap."

He chuckled, rubbing his hands down her back. "Showering isn't as much fun without you there."

When he lowered his voice and gazed into her eyes, she was tempted to give him anything he wanted. But she'd come with Lauren. It wouldn't be right to make her friend drive home alone. Still, she found herself tempted. She reached up on tiptoes and brushed a kiss against his lips. "I'll see what I can arrange."

"I'll make it worth it for you."

A languid heat filled her limbs and an ove whelming need to be close to him rose inside h Her heart skittered and Stacie knew she had to the situation under control or she'd end up d something foolish. She took a deep breath focused on the box. "If you take that side, I'll

Josh reached around her and lifted the entire box without any trouble. "I'll carry. You open the door. Deal?"

She cleared her throat and found her voice. "Deal."

On the walk to the house Stacie found herself distracted by the intoxicating scent of his cologne and the heat emanating from his strong, work-hardened body.

How could she ever have believed the starving-poet look was sexy? Such a man could never have handled the cake in such an efficient manner. Or, for that matter, rescued her from the clutches of a vicious serpent...

"My snake bite is all better." She climbed the steps without the slightest twinge of discomfort and held the screen door open for him. "If not for the fang marks, I'd think that day had been just a bad dream."

"Not all of it was bad." Josh paused for a moment in the doorway, his gaze raking over her body. "I got to see you naked for the first time."

He flashed a smile and stepped into the house, leaving her to stamp out the flames of desire his words had reignited.

An hour later, when she took her seat at one of the tables Seth had set up, the embers still smoldered. She tried to focus on the food, but it wasn't easy. Not with Josh beside her.

Seth had furnished barbeque beef for the potluck while the guests were to bring a variety of dishes. Since this was Stacie's first party in Sweet River,

she'd been determined to bring something exciting and different. Thankfully, several nights earlier, a strawberry and feta salad had come to life in her head.

She'd reworked the ingredients multiple times, intent on getting the balance of flavors and textures perfect. Once she was satisfied, she'd had her room-mates do a taste test. Anna raved about the toasted almonds. Lauren, who didn't even like feta cheese, had given the dish an A+.

"Anyone know who brought the salad with the strawberries and almonds?" Seth glanced around the table. "It's really good."

"That would be me." Lauren's cheeks turned a becoming shade of pink when Seth focused his at-tention on her. "Actually Stacie made it, but I brought it into the house."

"A team effort," Seth said, a teasing glint in his eyes.

"With her doing 99.9% and me doing the rest," Lauren responded in an equally light tone.

"Each member of a team is important," Seth said.

Stacie listened to the banter in amazement. If she didn't know better, she'd think Lauren was flirting with Anna's brother. Could scholarly Lauren really have the hots for a man who rode horses and worked with his hands?

The answer was like a rolling pin up the side of her head. *Absolutely not.*

"You're right, Seth," Anna chimed in. "This salad is fabulous. Like I told Stacie, if she enters this recipe, she'll win the contest for sure."

"Contest?" Josh's fork paused midair.

Stacie shot her roommate a warning look. But Anna must not have seen it because she leaned forward, her voice loud enough that everyone at the table could easily hear.

"I read about it in the *Denver Post*." Excitement reverberated in Anna's voice. "Best recipe wins five thousand dollars *and* a chance to work for Jivebread."

"Jivebread?" Seth grabbed two corn muffins from a basket on the table. He kept one for himself and lobbed the other across the table to Josh, who caught it easily. "Never heard of it."

"It's one of the top catering firms in Denver," Anna explained. "Working there has always been Stacie's dream."

Josh lowered his fork and though Stacie didn't glance his way, she could feel his eyes on her.

"I think she's got an excellent chance at winning," Lauren added. "*If* she enters by next week's deadline."

The baked beans that had been sliding quite nicely down Stacie's throat came to an abrupt halt. She swallowed hard.

"Why wouldn't she enter?" Seth said. "This salad is her ticket to the top."

Her roommates had said the same thing at least a hundred times. Stacie knew they didn't understand her hesitation. Heck, she didn't fully understand it herself.

The entry fee was reasonable. And even if Abbie and Marc hadn't liked her previous recipes, that didn't mean they wouldn't like this one. This truly was, or could be, her chance to grab the brass ring.

Stacie ignored Josh's questioning glance and focused on the food on her plate. Thankfully everyone at the table seemed eager to talk and the conversation flowed to the next topic.

Seth told stories from his little girl Danica's childhood. Lauren updated everyone on the number of surveys she'd processed to date. And Anna brought out some new clothing designs she'd "just happened" to bring along for everyone to ooh and aah over.

Dressed in a frilly pink "princess" dress, Dani flitted from room to room, her blue eyes sparkling and an infectious smile on her lips. When the seven-year-old wasn't playing with her friends or bestowing wishes with her "magic wand," she was begging her dad to let her blow out her birthday candles.

"Fifteen minutes." Seth promised. His smile widened as his gaze lingered on the sparkly tiara Anna had placed on his daughter's blond head. "Our guests are still eating dinner."

"But Daddy, I want my cake and ice cream now. Pleaaase—"

"Danica." Seth's firm tone left no room for argument. "One more word and I'll make it twenty."

The child studied him for a long second and then heaved an exaggerated sigh worthy of any princess.

Anna pushed back her chair and stood. She held out a hand to her niece. "Fifteen minutes is just enough time for one game of musical chairs."

Danica's expression immediately brightened. "I'll get Madison and Emily and Tyler and Jessie." She took off running, still spouting names.

Lauren rose to her feet. "I'll help."

"I'll take you up on that offer," Anna said to Lauren before slanting a glance at her brother. "Just make sure you have the cake ready to cut in fifteen."

Seth appeared not to hear, but seconds later he disappeared into the kitchen, leaving Stacie and Josh alone at the table.

"I probably should help," Stacie said, making no move to get up.

"You've done your part." Josh placed his hand over hers and gave it a quick squeeze. "Relax and enjoy the evening."

"I am enjoying it," Stacie admitted.

Josh shifted, turning in his chair to face her. "You sound surprised."

"I didn't have any idea what this would be like." Stacie's lips lifted in a rueful smile. "I never expected so many people to attend a child's birthday party."

"In this part of the country, any occasion is a reason for a party." Josh took a sip of iced tea. "My parents would have been here, but my dad wasn't feeling well."

Recently there had been times when Stacie had wondered about his parents; what they were like, whether she'd like them, whether they'd like her. Though it didn't matter, she *was* curious.

His mother had given the blue heeler to her son, so she was obviously an animal lover. She and Stacie would have that in common. And despite any misgivings, his father had supported his son's decision to be a rancher, which told her she'd like him, too.

"I'm sorry to hear they won't be here," Stacie said. "It would have been nice to meet them."

"They were looking forward to meeting you," Josh said. "They've heard so much about you."

Stacie stilled. "From you?"

Josh shook his head. "Everyone but me."

She lifted a questioning brow.

"Word on the street is that Anna's friend has taken up with their son," he said, answering her unspoken question.

"I hope you set them straight," Stacie said. "Made sure they understand we're just good friends."

"I did mention you and Lauren and Anna will be moving back to Denver soon," Josh said.

"I'm not sure about *soon,* but you're right, that time will be here before we know it." Stacie tried to summon some enthusiasm. Two months ago she'd have given anything to return to Denver. But that was before Josh. "I'll have to find another apartment. Another job—"

"You'll have a job," Josh said. "Once you win the contest."

"To win, I have to enter."

Josh grinned. "That's usually the way it works."

"I'm not sure I'm going to enter." Stacie traced an imaginary figure eight on the lace tablecloth with one finger. "Every time I think of mailing the entry I get this scared feeling in the pit of my stomach."

Josh searched her eyes—for what, she wasn't

certain—but whatever he found there must have satisfied him because he accepted her explanation without comment and changed the subject. "Do you like porch swings?"

Stacie smiled. "Love 'em."

"Good," he said. "'cause that's where we're headed."

She followed his lead and stood, but she hesitated when he offered his hand.

Though she knew Seth had kept his mouth shut after their first night together, the fact that she and Josh were spending so much time together had caused some raised eyebrows. From the knowing glances being cast their way this evening, the gossip mill appeared poised to grind out innuendoes and rumors at breakneck speed.

Yet, something in Josh's eyes told her she'd hurt him more by ignoring his hand. She wrapped her fingers around his and let him lead her to the porch swing. She took a seat on the far right. He plopped down in the middle and without either of them saying a word, they began to swing.

The back-and-forth motion was soothing, almost hypnotic. And when Josh slipped an arm around her shoulders and tugged her close, a feeling of complete and utter contentment stole over Stacie.

Billowy clouds wrapped the sky in a thick blanket of gray, muting the normal nighttime sounds. Laughter and conversation drifted through the screen door, but seemed far away. She and Josh were alone in the moment.

In the past, Stacie would have been bored and eager to get back to the party. But she wasn't as restless as she used to be. Sitting in the twilight with Josh at her side was enough.

"Tell me why you're hesitating," he said in a low tone that invited confidences. "What's holding you back from entering that contest?"

This was it. Her opportunity to tell him what being in Sweet River had meant to her. Her chance to make him understand that she loved small-town life, her work at the café and most of all…him.

But she hesitated. Though she was pretty sure he loved her, he'd never said the words and she couldn't bring herself to go first. So she played it safe and told the story he already knew, the one she'd been telling for years.

"When I started tenth grade, my parents started telling me how important it was to have a plan for my future." Stacie chuckled. "But to have a plan, you have to know what you want to do. I knew I didn't want to work with numbers like my mother. Or own an auto dealership like my dad. And I certainly didn't want to follow my oldest brother and go to law school."

They swung in silence for several long seconds.

"I wanted to do something creative, something fun," Stacie said. "I told them I wanted to find my bliss."

"What did they say?"

"They didn't *say* anything," Stacie said. "They laughed."

"You didn't let that dissuade you."

"In a way I did," Stacie said with a sigh. "I got a

BA in business. I put my dreams on hold for four years."

"Then you were free to pursue your dreams."

"Yes. But my bliss hasn't been as easy to find as I thought," Stacie admitted.

Until I came here and met you, she thought.

The expression on Josh's face changed, and for a second she feared she'd spoken aloud.

"What about Jivebread?" he asked.

"That type of place would be my ideal job. The company prides itself on its unique cuisine. If I worked for them I'd be encouraged to develop new recipes, as well as prepare and serve the food."

"Sounds...busy."

"I'm sure it is," Stacie said. "But like with anything, if you enjoy what you're doing, it doesn't seem like work."

She thought of the time she spent making her rolls and breads for the Coffee Pot. The hours she'd put in helping Merna get her accounting and ordering systems organized. It had been a labor of love.

"I'd have thought you'd be working for them by now."

"I applied several times. I got the interview, but I didn't have enough relevant experience. I even offered to start at the bottom. Still no cigar." Stacie remembered how upset she'd been. But if she'd gotten that job, she wouldn't be here with Josh now.

"So this contest would be your ticket in."

Stacie reluctantly nodded. "*If* I win."

Josh lifted an eyebrow. "You have doubts?"

"The last thing Paul said to me before he left was that a smart person knows when to shut the door on a dream." She knew Paul was trying to tell her she should stop searching for her bliss. But over the past couple of weeks Stacie's heart had also been telling her that she could quit. The bliss she'd longed for couldn't be found working for Jivebread in Denver. It was here, with Josh. "I've been thinking that maybe I should just find a normal job, get married and forget about Jivebread."

"What are you saying?"

"Maybe I should stay here in Montana…with you."

Chapter Fourteen

For a moment, Josh stared, unable to believe this wonderful woman wanted to stay in Sweet River with him. His heart pumped hard in his chest.

"Ah, Stacie." He pulled her to him, needing to feel her body against his, needing the reassurance that she was with him now and that's where she wanted to stay.

This was what he'd hoped for ever since he'd fallen in love with her. He wanted her to choose to live in Sweet River. Not because she was scared to face the outside world or because she didn't have other options, but because she loved the land and people as much as he did.

She snuggled close. "Who needs Jivebread anyway?"

An icy chill formed a tight fist of doubt around Josh's heart. He rubbed his hands up and down her back, telling himself that she wouldn't regret her decision to live here. He'd make her so happy she'd forget about her dreams.

She'd forget about her dreams.

The realization was like a kick to his gut. That was the lie he'd told himself when he'd married Kristin. Her major in college had been broadcast journalism, and everyone agreed she was born to be in front of a camera.

But the year they'd graduated, jobs in her field had been scarce. The world she'd envisioned had failed to materialize. He hadn't realized it at the time, but he'd been her consolation prize.

He'd had reservations when she suggested they get married, after all. Every time he'd brought her home she couldn't wait to get back to the city. But she convinced him—and he hadn't been that hard to convince—that once Sweet River was her home things would be different.

Trouble was, it hadn't been different. She'd hated the land, the people and, in time, him. And she'd blamed him for cheating her out of her dream. In a way, Josh understood. He'd known how much her chosen career meant to her, yet he'd let her give it up.

Wouldn't a man who truly loved a woman do everything possible to make sure she was happy? Wouldn't he encourage her to follow her dreams even if those dreams didn't include him? Wouldn't a man in love help the woman he loved find her bliss?

According to her friends, Stacie had wanted the position at Jivebread for years. Yet, like Kristin, she professed a willingness to give it all up...for him.

It hadn't worked for Kristin. Why would it work for Stacie?

"I'd like it if you stayed here. Heck, who am I kidding, I'd love it." Josh brushed a kiss against her hair, fighting the raw emotion rising inside him. He took a moment and cleared his throat. "But you should enter the contest anyway."

Stacie lifted her head from his chest and he could see the confusion in her eyes. "What would be the point?"

"The salad you brought to Dani's party was a culinary masterpiece," Josh said. "It deserves a chance to shine."

You deserve a chance to shine, he thought.

Her gaze lingered on his face. "Why is having me enter that contest such a big deal to everyone?"

Because everyone knows that getting that job is what you need, what you want, what you deserve, he wanted to say.

"Humor us. Humor me," he said instead, keeping his tone light. "Put the entry in the mail."

"I'll do it." She wrapped her arms around his neck and smiled. "But in exchange, I get to see you naked."

Josh fulfilled his part of the deal and Stacie mailed the entry the next day. In the ensuing weeks she forgot about it. Putting the contest out of her mind wasn't hard when every day seemed to bring something new and exciting.

With Merna's blessing, Stacie started a gourmet dinner night at the Coffee Pot. Though Merna warned her that once the café sold the event would likely end, Stacie decided to have fun with it. The five-course menu was a big hit with the dude-ranch guests, as well as the locals. A food critic from the *Billings Gazette* proclaimed her brisket with apricots and lemon juice "the best in the state."

Lauren's dissertation research continued to bring like-minded individuals together. Sasha and Wes were both matched, but not to each other. Misty was paired with a rancher who lived outside of Big Timber. Stacie knew that relationship was destined for success when she heard they'd sung a karaoke duet at Earl's Saturday night.

Stacie continued to spend most of her free time with Josh. The only downside was she barely saw her roommates. That's why she'd asked Anna to pick huckleberries with her this morning.

The excursion was the perfect opportunity for some serious girl talk. Not to mention that when Anna started reciting all the uses for the berries, Stacie's mind had immediately began flipping the pages of her mental cookbook.

She could already taste the pan-seared chicken breast with huckleberries, blue cheese and port sauce. The dish would make a fabulous entrée for the Coffee Pot's next gourmet night. Of course, she'd be sure to set aside enough berries to make a pie, and

maybe even use some to make compote for her increasingly popular buttermilk biscuits, which now
rivaled her cinnamon rolls.

As her mind explored all the possibilities, she
plucked berries and placed them gently into a basket.
In the distance birds cawed and the leaves of a large
cottonwood whispered in the breeze. A feeling of
contentment stole over Stacie. She couldn't remember ever being so happy.

She had her cooking, her friends and Josh.
Though she hadn't thought it possible, every day
she loved him more. Only one thing troubled her.
"Do you know Josh has never told me he loves
me?"

"Buckets of blood." The curse shot from Anna's
mouth, and she slowly straightened, hand pressed
against her lower spine. "I feel like a ninety-year-old
granny with rheumatism."

Stacie had to smile, both at her friend's long-
suffering expression and at the phrase. Anna had
done nothing but complain since they started picking. Even if you ignored the fact that her chartreuse
sling-backs were totally unsuitable for a day in the
woods, the country girl was clearly out of her ele-
ment—even if she'd spent her childhood in this kind
of life.

"Did you hear what I said?" Stacie asked when
Anna started mumbling something about a hot tub
and massage.

Anna stopped and turned, shading her eyes with
her hand. "Your back hurts, too?"

"My back is fine," Stacie said. "My problem is Josh."

"I thought you two were doing great." Anna's brows pulled together. Stacie could hear the surprise in her voice.

"He hasn't said he loves me," Stacie said, embarrassed by the admission yet not sure why. "Don't you find that strange?"

"Why would you even expect it?" Anna asked, her expression clearly puzzled. "You said it was just a physical thing between the two of you."

Stacie shifted uneasily from one foot to the other.

Anna's gaze narrowed. "Is there something you're not telling me?"

Stacie could feel her face warm. "The physical thing didn't work."

"What?" Anna's mouth dropped open. "Josh can't—?"

"No, no, nothing like that." Stacie hesitated to explain. "I went into this with the best of intentions. I just couldn't keep it strictly physical." Stacie heaved a sigh. "I guess I'm not a fling kind of girl."

Anna chuckled. "That doesn't surprise me at all."

"I love him, Anna. Truly. Deeply. Completely." A lump rose and lodged in Stacie's throat. "I'm just not sure how he feels."

Her friend didn't appear at all shocked by the admission. She brought a finger to her lips. "What did he say when you told him you love him?"

Stacie rolled her eyes. Had the sun affected Anna's brain? "Women don't say 'I love you' first."

Anna laughed. "What century are you living in?"

"I have it on very good authority that the man should declare his love first."

"What good authority is that?"

"My mother."

"The same mother who told you not to sleep with a guy because no one wants to buy the cow when the milk is free?" Anna's lips twitched. "You didn't seem to have any problem not following that suggestion."

Anna shot her a leer that was so over the top that Stacie couldn't help but chuckle.

"Some of her advice may be a bit dated," Stacie admitted. "But what if I say 'I love you' and he just stares at me? What if there's a horribly awkward silence?"

"What if he takes you into his arms and says he loves you, too?"

"You're probably right." Stacie had told herself over and over that her fears were unfounded and foolish. With his every look, every gesture, every touch, Josh declared his love. "I'm making a big deal out of nothing."

"What are you going to do about it?"

"I'm—"

"I thought I'd never find you two." Lauren stumbled through the brush. Sweat dotted her brow and her white cotton shirt had twigs stuck to it. "I finally called Seth and he told me this used to be a favorite spot of yours."

Although Anna didn't act surprised, Lauren was

the last person Stacie expected to see this morning. Stacie shot Lauren a curious gaze. "I thought you told us you were too busy analyzing your data to pick berries?"

"Hey, don't look a gift horse in the mouth. Put her to work." Anna gestured to the bushes brimming with berries. "Grab a basket, Lauren, and start picking."

"I didn't come for the berries." Lauren pulled a thin white envelope out of her bag and offered it to Stacie. "I came to give you this."

Stacie placed her basket on the ground and wiped her hands on her jeans. "What is it?"

"It's from the contest." Lauren shoved the paper into Stacie's hand.

Stacie stared at the return address. As she focused on the Jivebread logo, her heart tap-danced in her chest. The light-as-a-feather envelope turned suddenly heavy in her hand.

"Open it," Anna urged.

Stacie took a deep breath. How many years had she dreamed of working for Jivebread? Of working in a state-of-the-art kitchen with any ingredients she could imagine at her disposal. Of working with other professionals who understood the thrill of creating with food. A shiver traveled up her spine, but she stopped the rising excitement by reminding herself that dream was before Josh. "I'll look at this later."

"Aren't you curious?" Lauren's gaze remained focused on the envelope. "Don't you want to know what it says?"

"Yeah." Anna crowded close, leaning over Stacie's shoulder. "The past three weeks have been pure torture. I can't wait another minute."

It was Stacie's letter. She could take it back to the house. Open it only when she was good and ready. But Stacie knew her roommates wouldn't give her a moment's peace until she did.

With a resigned sigh, Stacie slipped open the envelope and pulled out a sheet of crisp parchment paper. A check fluttered to the ground. She read the words silently once. Then read them again just to be sure.

"How did you do?" Anna asked.

"What does it say?" Lauren added.

A sense of wonder flowed through Stacie's veins. She lifted her gaze. "I won."

Chapter Fifteen

By the time the three women arrived back at the house, Stacie felt drunk with compliments. After years of honing her skills, her talent had been recognized by professionals. That was an even better gift than the five-thousand-dollar check.

She and Anna placed baskets of huckleberries on the back porch and then formed an impromptu conga line behind Lauren and danced their way to the dining room.

"This is just so cool," Anna said for the tenth—or was it the hundredth?—time. "And to think you almost didn't enter."

"I'm glad we pushed you." A self-satisfied smile tipped the corners of Lauren's lips.

Stacie didn't bother to correct her friends, but she knew it was *Josh's* encouragement that had made the difference. It was as if he knew winning the contest would give her a much-needed boost in self-confidence. And the money, well, she already had a plan for it…

"Time for a toast," Anna declared, uncorking the bottle of champagne Lauren had picked up on their way back into town.

Lauren grabbed three crystal wineglasses from the antique china cabinet. She'd just finished filling the glasses when the doorbell rang.

"I wonder who that is?" Stacie asked.

Lauren and Anna exchanged glances.

"Surely you didn't think we were going to have a celebration of this magnitude with just the three of us?" Anna asked with a smile.

Lauren pulled two more glasses from the cabinet.

Stacie gave her friend an assessing look. "Who did you invite?"

Lauren filled the extra glasses, a tiny smile hovering on the edge of her lips. "I called Seth on my way home and asked him over. Josh was with him, so he's coming, too. I told them we had some celebrating to do."

Disappointment sluiced through Stacie. She knew Lauren meant well, but she'd wanted to tell Josh the news herself. "Oh."

"I didn't tell him *what* we were celebrating," Lauren hurriedly added. "That's your news to share."

"Anybody home?" Seth's voice rang through the

old house followed immediately by the clatter of boots on hardwood.

"Back here," Lauren called out.

Josh stopped next to Seth at the dining-room entrance. His gaze skipped over Anna and Lauren to settle on Stacie.

Even with her hair pulled back in a ponytail and a patch of dirt on one knee, she was the most beautiful woman he'd ever seen.

"Hey." Josh returned Stacie's smile, and then crossed the room to drape an arm around her shoulders. He found it increasingly hard to be near her and *not* touch her.

She lifted her face and Josh brushed a kiss across her lips, resisting the urge to linger. There'd be time for that later. "I didn't think I'd be seeing you until this evening."

"This is a special occasion." Lauren picked up two of the champagne glasses, handing one to Josh and another to Seth.

"It better be." Seth sounded gruff, but Josh knew his friend hadn't hesitated when Lauren had asked him over. "We were in the middle of branding when you called."

"Hold your spurs, cowboy," Anna said. "We wouldn't have asked you to come if it wasn't important."

Seth turned to Lauren. "Did you get all your survey participants? Is that what this is about?"

"Actually this is about me." When Stacie met Josh's gaze, it was as if she were speaking to him alone. "I won the contest."

"Congratulations," Seth said. "I knew that recipe was good."

Josh heard the pride in her voice, felt the excited tremble in her shoulders. The bliss she'd searched for all these years was now in reach, and he was happy for her. But the thought of losing her now filled him with regret and pain. He somehow managed to smile. "That's wonderful."

"This doesn't change anything," Stacie said in a low tone obviously meant to reassure him.

"I know that." He gave her shoulders a squeeze.

"This calls for a party," Seth said.

"My thoughts exactly." Lauren's eyes snapped with excitement.

"We'll have it here at the house," Anna mused aloud, and Josh could almost see her mind kick into high gear.

"It'll be a send-off the likes of which this town has never seen." Lauren lifted her glass.

"But I'm not—" Stacie began.

"To Stacie." Seth raised his glass. "To continued success."

Josh joined in the toast. If he was honest with himself he'd admit this was the worst news he'd ever received, far uglier than Kristin's request for a divorce. But he kept his thoughts to himself and managed to talk and laugh as if this were the best news he'd ever heard.

It was funny. He'd never known he had a talent for acting…until now.

* * *

Stacie wasn't surprised when Josh made up an excuse to cancel their date. She'd seen the look of surprise in his eyes when she'd made her announcement. She'd felt him pull away even as he stood beside her.

She'd wanted to reassure him that this changed nothing between them, but he left with Seth before she had the chance. He hadn't even kissed her goodbye.

"This party is going to be fabulous." Lauren glanced up from the list of names she and Anna had been compiling since the men left.

"I'm so glad you'll be back in Denver before us." Anna added another name to the list before looking up. "That way we'll have a place to live once Lauren's work here is done."

"This is a dream come true." Lauren heaved a happy sigh. "I remember you talking about working for Jivebread and now it's happening. When do you start?"

"Anytime during this next month," Stacie said automatically, recalling the instructions in the letter. "It's up to me. Assuming I want to work for Jivebread."

"Of course you do," Anna said.

"Actually, I don't." Stacie pulled a chair back from the table and took a seat opposite her friends. "I'm not moving back to Denver. I'm staying here in Sweet River with Josh."

Anna's pencil paused midword. Lauren opened her mouth then shut it. Finally Anna leaned forward, resting her forearms on the table.

"This is what you've been searching for your entire life." Anna took a deep breath then slowly released it. "I adore Josh, but opportunities like this only come around once. If you walk away now, it's gone. How can you think of giving up your dream for a guy who hasn't even told you he loves you?"

Lauren raised an eyebrow. "Really?"

"He does love me." Stacie shoved back her chair and stood. She'd thought her friends would understand. "Just because he hasn't said it doesn't mean—"

"You want that job," Lauren said. "I can see it in your eyes."

"Of course I want it," Stacie explained. "I just want Josh more."

"I realize you've fallen in love with this area and with Josh—" Anna spoke slowly and deliberately "—but how are you going to feel when Lauren and I are back in Denver, the snow is piled high and ranch life isn't quite what you envisioned?"

"I love Josh," Stacie repeated, more forcefully this time. "And I love it here."

"Would you stay if he didn't love you back?" Lauren asked.

The very suggestion that Josh might not return her feelings tore at Stacie's heartstrings. Could she stay in Sweet River loving him, knowing he didn't love her back?

She shook her head. "I think it would be too hard."

"You know what you have to do." Lauren's eyes were clear and very green.

Stacie met Lauren's gaze, but couldn't make herself speak.

"Before you make your final decision, before you throw away something you won't be able to get back," Lauren said, her gaze as pointed as her words, "you need to find out how he feels about you."

Josh grabbed a bottle of beer from the refrigerator and took it to the living room. He clicked on the television, but minutes later muted the sound, irritated by the sitcom laugh track.

What a difference a few hours could make. This morning he'd jumped out of bed, anticipation fueling his steps. After he helped Seth, he'd looked forward to the evening with Stacie. Instead, one piece of mail had changed her life and his...forever. Stacie would soon be gone and he doubted he'd ever see her again.

Unless I tell her I love her, he said to himself.

Part of him wanted to hop into his truck, head straight back to Anna's house and tell Stacie he loved her more than he'd ever thought possible. But the other part refused to let him act on that impulse. If Stacie stayed in Sweet River, it had to be *her* decision, not one he influenced with three little words.

Josh took a long sip of beer, wishing it were strong enough to stifle the pain in his heart. But then again, there wasn't enough alcohol in the world to accomplish that impossible task.

The bottle found its way to his lips once again when the sound of a truck engine blended with Bert's barking. Josh glanced at the clock. Ten o'clock. Late for company to stop by.

Moving to the front window, Josh pushed back the curtain with one finger. His shoulders tensed at the sight of the Jeep.

By the time the bell rang he was in the foyer. He pulled open the door. "What a surprise."

"I don't see why." Stacie's chin tilted upward. "We had plans."

The wind lifted her hair from her shoulders. Thunder rumbled in the distance. Droplets of rain splattered the porch.

Josh opened the door wider and motioned her inside. When he touched her arm to move her aside so he could shut the door, her trembling caught him off guard.

"Are you okay?" He glanced out the front door but didn't see anything unusual. "Did something happen?"

"Hold me, Josh," she said. "I need to feel your arms around me."

If she'd asked him if he loved her, he had a non-committal response ready. If she pressed, he'd end up telling her the truth. And then he'd insist she pursue her dream before committing to him. But her simple request caught him off guard. Before he could consider the full ramifications of his actions, he'd already wrapped his arms around her and pulled her close.

They fit together perfectly.

Like we were made to be together, he thought.

Josh shoved the fanciful thought aside but couldn't keep from reveling in the feel of her body against his. The scent of jasmine filled his nostrils and he knew he'd never be able to smell that scent without thinking of her.

He wasn't sure how long they stood there, the house silent except for their hearts beating in perfect rhythm. The light from the living room cast a warm glow. It was as if they were alone in their own world.

Stacie rested her head against his chest. "Tonight I want us to play a game of 'Let's Pretend.'"

Josh opened his mouth to turn her down, but those words wouldn't come. "What do you want to pretend?"

"That for now, *for right now,* there's only you and me." Stacie met his gaze. "I need to be close to you."

The desperation in her eyes told him that she knew that tonight could be their last time. Making love would be a way of saying goodbye. For him, it would also be his way of showing his love.

His feelings were strong and deep and true. Whatever he'd felt for Kristin had been a pale imitation of what he felt for the woman standing before him.

"Okay." He lifted his hands and tilted her head back, brushing tears from her cheeks with the pads of his thumbs. "Okay."

She smiled tremulously as he captured her hand and led her to the bedroom.

"Oh, Josh." Stacie breathed the words.

For a second, he wasn't sure what had made her

eyes shine until he saw the bed. This morning, in anticipation of the evening ahead, he'd scattered red rose petals across the sheets. While he'd never been a romantic guy, lately he'd found himself looking for out-of-the-ordinary ways to make Stacie happy.

She touched his arm. "You are so sweet."

"And you are so beautiful." Josh's lips moved lightly across her mouth then trailed down her cheek to bury in the warm fragrance of her neck.

Though he was starved for her, he forced himself to take his time. He sipped from her lips, rather than gulped. He moved his hands gently over her curves, asking rather than demanding.

Slow and easy, he told himself. Memories of this night would have to last a lifetime.

The moon cast a golden glow through the open window. As they kissed, her sighs of pleasure mingled with his.

"You have on way too many clothes," he muttered.

Stacie laughed and quickly rid herself of her jeans and shirt. Seconds later she stood naked before him, hands on hips. "Now who's the one who's overdressed?"

Josh winked. "Not for long."

He jerked his shirt over his head and tossed it aside. His jeans and boxers had barely hit the floor when he gently pushed her down on the bed and lay beside her.

Stacie ran her hands over his biceps then trailed them over his chest. They'd made love numerous times before, but somehow this felt new. "So strong, so—"

"Soft." He cupped her breasts in his palms, his fingers brushing the tips. Her nipple puckered and tingled as he continued his exploration, skipping his hands over intimate dips and hollows.

Stacie sighed. His touch was gentle and caring. The silky thickness of his hair brushed against her breast. Stacie slid her hands across his shoulders, up through his hair. It had never been clearer. A lifetime with this wonderful man wouldn't be nearly long enough.

"Joshua." She put everything she felt, all the love and longing in her heart, into that single word.

His lips closed over hers once more, his tongue plunging into her mouth with a hunger at odds with the gentle pressure of his hand between her legs.

She responded fully, without reservation. Her passion, her need for him, grew with each kiss, each tender caress. Finally she couldn't stand it anymore. She needed to have him fill her so completely that nothing could come between them. "I want you. Now."

A second later he thrust inside her, and Stacie groaned with pleasure. His strokes lengthened, quickened. Wrapping her arms around him she moved her body in an age-old rhythm. She loved the way he felt inside her, rubbing her intimately, filling her.

Stacie rode the building pressure until their bodies were damp and sweaty. Still she clung to him. He was the sexiest man in the world to her, and he was all hers. And when the combination of emotion and physical sensation sent her crashing over the edge, it was right that she was in his arms when the world exploded.

When Stacie returned to earth, a smile of pure pleasure lifted her lips. "That was incredible."

Without taking his eyes off her, Josh lifted her hand to his mouth and pressed a kiss in the palm. "*You* are incredible."

She leaned her head against his hand. The raw emotion rising inside her refused to be contained. "I love you, Josh. I love you so very much."

Josh froze. His smile disappeared and his eyes grew shuttered. The awkward silence she'd envisioned never occurred because he jumped up so quickly you'd have thought the barn was on fire.

"I'll make us something to eat." Snatching his clothes from the floor, Josh exited the bedroom without a backward glance.

For several seconds, Stacie lay motionless, stunned. He didn't love her. A fling, that's all she was to him. She blinked back the tears that flooded her eyes. She would not cry. She. Would. Not. Cry.

Though her chest was so tight she could barely breathe, Stacie dressed quickly. She stopped only to swipe at tears that seemed determined to fall.

She could hear Josh clanging pans in the kitchen when she reached the front door. She thought about saying goodbye. But she was too busy for meaningless conversation with her summer fling. She had a move to Denver to arrange.

Chapter Sixteen

Josh sat in the pew next to his parents and wondered what craziness had made him agree to attend Sunday services. Granted, his mother was being honored for her years as Sunday School superintendent, but he could have come up with a believable excuse.

He'd been working hard, too hard if you listened to his father. But there was a lot to do on a ranch this time of year. And Josh had discovered when he pushed himself physically, by the time he got home he was too exhausted to do much more than collapse into bed. Which was exactly how he wanted it.

No time to think. No time to miss Stacie. No time to wonder if he'd made the biggest mistake of his life.

He'd hoped the pain would lessen with each passing day. Instead it had grown worse. He remembered the sweet love they'd made, the look in Stacie's eyes when she'd told him she loved him, the strength it had taken not to say the words back.

Because he did love her. More than he ever thought possible. In fact, he'd give up everything to be with her now....

Whoa. The thought took him by surprise, but he couldn't deny the joy had gone out of his life when Stacie left. Like his father always said: all the treasures in the world don't mean much without someone you love by your side.

When Kristin left, Josh felt she'd failed to live up to her promise. She'd told him she wanted to live in Montana, and then, after they were married, she'd changed her mind. What he hadn't realized until this moment was that he'd failed her, too.

Not once had he seriously considered giving up his life on the ranch to move to where she could find work in her field. If he'd loved Kristin the way a man should love his wife, he'd have gone to the ends of the earth with her...

"Wasn't that a wonderful sermon?" his mother whispered as they stood for the closing hymn.

"Yeah," Josh said, "it was great."

Truth was, he only heard bits and pieces of the sermon. Something about pursuing the life you want, not letting yourself be constrained by a spirit of fear...

He knew the life he wanted, and it was with

Stacie. Yet, he'd let her walk out of his life without a word of protest. Technically there was no reason she couldn't have her bliss and him, too. But for that to occur, he'd have to give up the land and the life he loved so much.

He'd never considered leaving for Kristin. But for Stacie…

Could he do it? Could he walk away from his legacy and not look back? Did he really love her that much?

Though it was late when Stacie returned to her hotel room, she headed straight for her laptop.

She kicked off her shoes while the computer booted up. In the three weeks she'd been in Denver, reading e-mail from Sweet River had become her reward at the end of long, stress-filled days.

The work at Jivebread had exciting moments, but Stacie felt detached from the customers she served. Not like in Sweet River, where she cooked and baked for the people she cheered alongside at baseball games and worshipped with on Sunday.

She'd called Anna and Lauren last Friday at a particularly low point. They'd been surprised she was having so much difficulty acclimating. Go out with coworkers, they'd urged. Check out a new movie. Join a gym.

Stacie hadn't been able to make them understand that she didn't have the heart to do any of those things. Heaving a sigh, Stacie scanned her in-box.

She read the e-mails from Lauren and Anna first.

Anna had finally been matched. Lauren was ecstatic. Anna was reserving judgment until she met the guy.

Stacie opened the e-mail from Merna next.

Dear Stacie,

I can't believe it's been almost a month since you left. Every day at least one person asks when you'll be back. The owners of the dude ranches are pressuring me to restart the gourmet meal night. I'd like to, but I don't have your talent for planning or preparing that kind of food.

You asked if I'd found a buyer for the café yet. Unfortunately the answer is no. Earl Jenkins has expressed interest, but he wants to turn it into a bar. Just what Sweet River needs...another watering hole! lol

I really don't want to sell to him, but my daughter needs me. If I go much longer without an offer, I may not have a choice.

I hope all is well with you.

Love, Merna

Stacie sat back in her chair and massaged the bridge of her nose. She couldn't imagine Sweet River without a café. She shifted her gaze back to her in-box. A new message from AlexD caught her eye. She opened it next.

Dear Stacie,

I hope you don't mind that I got your e-mail address from your roommates. I wanted to let you know how grateful I am for the advice you gave me at the baseball game. When you told me I should become more involved and visible in the community I was skeptical. But you were right. I picked up a few clients by frequenting the barbershop. But when I joined a dart league at Earl's, business really took off. I realize a dart league sounds rather pedestrian, but I'm enjoying it.

I was surprised to hear you'd left Sweet River— you and the town seemed perfectly suited—but I wish you only the best in your new endeavor.

Sincerely,
Alexander Darst, Esq.

"I sometimes wonder why I left, too," Stacie murmured. But even as the words left her lips, she knew the answer.

Shoving Josh's image from her mind she returned her attention to the lengthy list of unopened mail.

A message from her brother had sat unopened for several days. She started to click on it, but the growling in her stomach reminded her she hadn't eaten since lunch. So she clicked on the MP3 file of Pastor Barbee's sermon instead. Turning up the volume, she headed for the refrigerator.

The sermons had shown up in her in-box every Monday since she'd left Sweet River. She wasn't sure how the church had gotten her e-mail address, but it didn't really matter.

While she'd been tempted to erase the first, once she listened she'd been hooked. When Pastor Barbee preached all she had to do was close her eyes and she was back in Sweet River, surrounded by the people and the land she loved. Just thinking of the meadows filled with flowers and the smell of fresh-mown hay brought a tightness to her throat.

Shoving the emotion aside, Stacie opened the refrigerator and pulled out some carrots and celery while the sermon continued. The reverend had chosen a verse from Timothy, something about not having a spirit of fear. As his words continued to fill the room, it was as if he were speaking directly to *her.* She'd left the only place that'd ever felt like home because she was scared. Scared of living near the man she loved, knowing he would never be hers. Scared she'd see him on the street and not know what to say. Scared of hurting even more than she did now.

By the time the sermon concluded, Stacie's head was spinning. She forced herself to concentrate and opened her brother's message. After skimming the paragraphs of family news, she read the rest more carefully.

...I'm so proud of you. Accepting the position with an up-and-coming company like Jivebread was a smart move. Though you never came out and said it, I know you were tempted to stay in that backwater town in Montana. I'm relieved you gave up the notion of finding your "bliss" and made a good business decision instead.

Stacie closed the e-mail, unable to read any more. Didn't Paul realize Jivebread *was* her bliss?

But if it's my bliss, shouldn't I be happy instead of miserable?

There was so much to like about Jivebread, so much to appreciate about Denver. But the truth was the Mile High City was no longer home to her.

With or without Josh, her heart, her bliss, was back in that small town in Montana. Now she had to decide if she had the courage to do something about it.

Chapter Seventeen

Traffic had been backed up on I-25. Unfortunately, when Stacie turned onto E470 it didn't improve. By the time she reached the Staybridge Suites on Tower Road, she was thirty minutes late for a dinner with a sorority sister she didn't remember.

Anna had told her that Josie Collier was in the process of moving to Denver after a heart-wrenching breakup in another state and needed a friend. Stacie had thought it might help cheer her up to eat at one of the bistros that had been popular during their college days. But Anna—acting as the intermediary—said Josie preferred to stay in and make dinner.

The extended-stay hotel where her former sorority sister was staying was similar to the one where

Stacie had been living. The lobby was warm and homey with overstuffed leather chairs and a large stone fireplace. She took the elevator to the third floor, following the signs to Suite 312.

Though Anna had insisted she didn't need to bring anything, Stacie refused to arrive empty-handed. She'd picked up a bottle of chardonnay when she learned through Anna that Josie was planning to serve fish.

Stacie stood at the door for a long moment, tension knotting her shoulders. This had been such a busy week with many loose ends to tie up. She really didn't feel like spending an evening making small talk with a woman she didn't remember.

But she reminded herself, it was the kindness of the strangers in Sweet River that had made such an impression, and this was her chance to pass such caring forward.

Plastering a smile on her face, Stacie gave the door a hard rap.

It swung open almost immediately and Stacie's breath caught in her throat. She blinked once. He didn't disappear. She blinked again. Still there.

Dressed in jeans and a chambray shirt, Josh Collins was thinner than she remembered. Lines of tension bracketed his mouth and the hollow look in his eyes was at odds with his bright smile. But he was still the handsomest cowboy she'd ever seen.

"Josh." Her voice sounded breathless to her ears. "What are you doing here?"

He took the bottle from her hands with hands that trembled slightly. "We'll open this later."

"We'll?" He was staying for dinner? Stacie's heart fluttered in her throat like a trapped butterfly as he motioned her inside. "This was supposed to be girl time." She glanced around the room. "Where's Josie?"

"Have a seat." He placed a hand on her arm and gestured with his head to a chair in the living room area. "I'll explain."

Her skin burned beneath his touch. Dear God, didn't he realize how hard this—

No. She stopped the thought before it could fully form. His unexpected appearance wasn't a disaster, but a blessing. When their paths crossed in the future, the initial awkwardness would be out of the way. They needed to have this conversation no matter how painful. But she really didn't want an audience.

"Where's Josie?" Stacie repeated in a voice loud enough to rouse the dead, but the woman still didn't appear.

"She doesn't exist." A sheepish look stole across his face. "It was a name Anna made up. Josie Collier. Josh Collins. Get it?"

Stacie stared at him for a long moment, confusion warring with a rising irritation. "What kind of game is this?"

"I wasn't sure you'd see me if I called," Josh said. "So I enlisted Anna's help."

"Meaning you got her to lie to me," Stacie said, her voice heavy with disappointment.

"I needed to talk to you." His gaze searched hers. "To tell you how I feel."

Stacie crossed her arms and cleared her throat. "You made your feelings—or shall I say lack of feelings—very clear the last time we were together."

"You walked out without a word."

Stacie lifted her chin. "You never came after me."

He hooked his thumbs in his belt loops and rocked back on his heels. "I wasn't going to be the only reason you stayed. I'd learned the hard way that sometimes love isn't enough. But I let you go and I'm an idiot."

By now Stacie was totally confused.

"I'd have stayed in Sweet River, if you'd asked," she found herself confessing when he didn't elaborate further.

"I wanted to," he said, and the regret in his voice took her by surprise. "But I knew what that position at Jivebread meant to you. I didn't want you to stay and later have regrets…like Kristin."

Now, finally, she understood. He'd deliberately made her think he didn't love her like she loved him. Stacie wanted to rail at him for the pain she'd endured. Tell him he had no right to make decisions for her. Tell him that he was wrong, that she could have remained in Sweet River and had no regrets. The trouble was she wasn't sure that was true. It had taken moving back to Denver to convince her that Sweet River was definitely where she belonged. She clasped her hands together to still their trembling. "Why are you here now?"

"I'm moving to Denver." He stepped closer and

took her hands in his, resisting her attempts to pull away. "I've come to ask for another chance. I thought my bliss was the Double C, but when you left I realized my happiness is wherever you are."

"You'd move here?" She must have misheard. "You can't be serious. What would happen to the ranch? And to Bert?"

He smiled. "I kinda hoped she could come with me. As for the ranch, one of my hired men has agreed to manage it for me. I'm thinking we should be able to get back every couple months to check on things."

Stacie shook her head, hoping the action would help her tangled thoughts make sense. "But what would you do here? In case you haven't noticed, there aren't any ranches or cattle nearby."

He shrugged, seemingly unconcerned. "I'll find something. What's important is we'll be together."

Stacie opened her mouth and then shut it. She frowned and slanted a glance in the direction of the kitchen. Was that a haze in the air? She sniffed. Then sniffed again. "Is something burning?"

An expletive shot from Josh's mouth, he sprinted to the stove. Stacie followed close behind. When he opened the oven door, smoke billowed out. Using a towel as an oven mitt, he pulled out a charred casserole.

By the time he'd placed it on the stovetop, Stacie had opened the window. She glanced over his shoulder and wrinkled her nose. "What is it? Or should I ask…what *was* it?"

Josh stared down at the crispy black contents with a crestfallen expression. "It *was* a tuna casserole."

"But you hate tuna."

He met Stacie's gaze. "I didn't make it for me."

Their gazes locked and her heart turned over. A warmth that had nothing to do with heat from the stove spread through her body. She finally understood why Josh had come. "You love me. Really and truly love me."

She couldn't keep the wonder from her voice. It all fit. Coming to Denver. Volunteering to give up his life in Sweet River. And now, the pièce de résistance: a tuna casserole.

"Of course I love you." Josh took her hands in his, his expression serious. "That's why I'm here. I love you and I want to marry you. If you'll have me."

It may not have been the fanciest proposal, but she could hear the sincerity in his voice, see the love in his eyes. The cowboy had put his heart on the line. The next step was hers.

The joyous answer rose from the deepest depths of Stacie's soul. "I'd be honored to be your wife."

The smile he shot her was blinding. "We're going to be very happy."

His hands slid up her arms. Though Stacie longed to melt against him, she took a step back. They would soon be starting a life together and she wanted no secrets between them.

"We *are* going to be happy," she said, "but you don't have to move to Denver for that to happen."

He cocked his head and she could see the puzzlement in his eyes.

"I'm moving back to Sweet River," she said. "Today was my last day at Jivebread."

A look of stunned disbelief crossed his face. "I don't understand," he said. "Working there was your passion—"

"My heart is in Sweet River." She gazed up at him. "It's where I belong. I was planning to return before you came to get me."

"Are you sure?"

"I've never been more sure of anything in my life," she said.

"I love you," he said, his voice husky and thick with emotion.

The words were music to her ears. Stacie knew that no matter how old she got or how many years passed that she'd never grow tired of hearing them. "Say it again."

"I love you." He pulled her close and planted kisses down her neck. "I love you. I love you."

She laughed with pure joy and Josh grinned. "Want me to show you how much?"

Though she couldn't wait to see what he had in mind, Stacie couldn't resist teasing. She widened her eyes. "You're going to make me another tuna casserole?"

"Another time," he promised. "For now, this will have to do."

As his lips closed over hers, Stacie had no doubt that this would do quite nicely indeed.

Epilogue

One year later

Stacie walked hand in hand with her husband down the main street in Sweet River, contentment draped around her like a favorite coat. "You remember what today is, don't you?"

A startled look skittered across Josh's face. "Our anniversary isn't until next month," he murmured to himself. "And it's not your birthday…"

"It's been a whole year since I moved back from Denver." What a wondrous day that had been, sunny and warm, but with a hint of fall in the air. When Josh had pulled into the lane leading to his house, she'd felt like a lost lamb who'd finally found her way home. "It's gone so fast."

"What do they say?" Josh grinned and shot her a wink. "Time flies when you're having fun?"

Stacie chuckled. It had been a fabulous, fun-filled twelve months. She and Josh had married less than a month after she returned in a simple but elegant ceremony in Anna's backyard. The quick wedding had given the town folk lots to talk about—and Lauren's research project a boost she hadn't anticipated.

Soon after, Stacie had become an entrepreneur like the rest of her family. She'd used the money she'd won in the contest as a down payment on the Coffee Pot, making her father and brother Paul proud.

Merna moved to California to be with her daughter. Shirley agreed to stay on and manage the café, giving Stacie time to bake and plan menus. Giving her time on the ranch with Josh. Giving them time to make the baby they both wanted.

Stacie's hand stole to her belly, which wouldn't be flat much longer. Tonight, before they met Josh's parents for dinner, she planned to tell him the good news.

"We like the new sign," Pastor Barbee commented as he and his wife strolled past the café, headed in the opposite direction. "Very eye-catching."

Stacie smiled at the couple. She'd worried how the community would react to changing the café's name to Bliss. So far she'd heard only positive comments.

Josh gave Stacie's hand a squeeze, his gaze focused on the sign he'd put up himself yesterday. "You've finally found your bliss."

Stacie let her gaze linger on the man who'd brought such joy to her life. Familiar, known, increasingly beloved, this cowboy was everything she'd ever wanted and more. Her heart overflowed with happiness and she leaned her head against his arm. "Yes, indeed. I've definitely found my bliss."

* * * * *

*Celebrate 60 years of pure reading pleasure
with Harlequin®!*
*Silhouette® Romantic Suspense is celebrating with
the glamour-filled, adrenaline-charged series*
LOVE IN 60 SECONDS *starting in April 2009.*
*Six stories that promise to bring the glitz of
Las Vegas, the danger of revenge, the mystery
of a missing diamond, family scandals and
ripped-from-the-headlines intrigue.
Get your heart racing as love happens in
sixty seconds!*

Enjoy a sneak peek of
USA TODAY *bestselling author
Marie Ferrarella's*
*THE HEIRESS'S 2-WEEK AFFAIR
Available April 2009
from Silhouette® Romantic Suspense.*

Eight years ago Matt Shaffer had vanished out of Natalie Rothchild's life, leaving behind a one-line note tucked under a pillow that had grown cold: *I'm sorry, but this just isn't going to work.*

That was it. No explanation, no real indication of remorse. The note had been as clinical and compassionless as an eviction notice, which, in effect, it had been, Natalie thought as she navigated through the morning traffic. Matt had written the note to evict her from his life.

She'd spent the next two weeks crying, breaking down without warning as she walked down the street, or as she sat staring at a meal she couldn't bring herself to eat.

Candace, she remembered with a bittersweet pang, had tried to get her to go clubbing in order to get her to forget about Matt.

She'd turned her twin down, but she did get her act together. If Matt didn't think enough of their relationship to try to contact her, to try to make her understand why he'd changed so radically from lover to stranger, then to hell with him. He was dead to her, she resolved. And he'd remained that way.

Until twenty minutes ago.

The adrenaline in her veins kept mounting.

Natalie focused on her driving. Vegas in the daylight wasn't nearly as alluring, as magical and glitzy as it was after dark. Like an aging woman best seen in soft lighting, Vegas's imperfections were all visible in the daylight. Natalie supposed that was why people like her sister didn't like to get up until noon. They lived for the night.

Except that Candace could no longer do that.

The thought brought a fresh, sharp ache with it.

"Damn it, Candy, what a waste," Natalie murmured under her breath.

She pulled up before the Janus casino. One of the three valets currently on duty came to life and made a beeline for her vehicle.

"Welcome to the Janus," the young attendant said cheerfully as he opened her door with a flourish.

"We'll see," she replied solemnly.

As he pulled away with her car, Natalie looked up

at the casino's logo. Janus was the Roman god with two faces, one pointed toward the past, the other facing the future. It struck her as rather ironic, given what she was doing here, seeking out someone from her past in order to get answers so that the future could be settled.

The moment she entered the casino, the Vegas phenomena took hold. It was like stepping into a world where time did not matter or even make an appearance. There was only a sense of "now."

Because in Natalie's experience she'd discovered that bartenders knew the inner workings of any establishment they worked for better than anyone else, she made her way to the first bar she saw within the casino.

The bartender in attendance was a gregarious man in his early forties. He had a quick, sexy smile, which was probably one of the main reasons he'd been hired. His name tag identified him as Kevin.

Moving to her end of the bar, Kevin asked, "What'll it be, pretty lady?"

"Information." She saw a dubious look cross his brow. To counter that, she took out her badge. Granted she wasn't here in an official capacity, but Kevin didn't need to know that. "Were you on duty last night?"

Kevin began to wipe the gleaming black surface of the bar. "You mean during the gala?"

"Yes."

The smile gracing his lips was a satisfied one. Last night had obviously been profitable for him, she judged. "I caught an extra shift."

She took out Candace's photograph and carefully placed it on the bar. "Did you happen to see this woman there?"

The bartender glanced at the picture. Mild interest turned to recognition. "You mean Candace Rothchild? Yeah, she was here, loud and brassy as always. But not for long," he added, looking rather disappointed. There was always a circus when Candace was around, Natalie thought. "She and the boss had at it and then he had our head of security escort her out."

She latched on to the first part of his statement. "They argued? About what?"

He shook his head. "Couldn't tell you. Too far away for anything but body language," he confessed.

"And the head of security?" she asked.

"He got her to leave."

She leaned in over the bar. "Tell me about him."

"Don't know much," the bartender admitted. "Just that his name's Matt Shaffer. Boss flew him in from L.A., where he was head of security for Montgomery Enterprises."

There was no avoiding it, she thought darkly. She was going to have to talk to Matt. The thought left her cold. "Do you know where I can find him right now?"

Kevin glanced at his watch. "He should be in his

office. On the second floor, toward the rear." He gave her the numbers of the rooms where the monitors that kept watch over the casino guests as they tried their luck against the house were located.

Taking out a twenty, she placed it on the bar. "Thanks for your help."

Kevin slipped the bill into his vest pocket. "Anytime, lovely lady," he called after her. "Anytime."

She debated going up the stairs, then decided on the elevator. The car that took her up to the second floor was empty. Natalie stepped out of the elevator, looked around to get her bearings and then walked toward the rear of the floor.

"'Into the Valley of Death rode the six hundred,'" she silently recited, digging deep for a line from a poem by Tennyson. Wrapping her hand around a brass handle, she opened one of the glass doors and walked in.

The woman whose desk was closest to the door looked up. "You can't come in here. This is a restricted area."

Natalie already had her ID in her hand and held it up. "I'm looking for Matt Shaffer," she told the woman.

God, even saying his name made her mouth go dry. She was supposed to be over him, to have moved on with her life. What happened?

The woman began to answer her. "He's—"

"Right here."

The deep voice came from behind her. Natalie felt every single nerve ending go on tactical alert at the same moment that all the hairs at the back of her neck stood up. Eight years had passed, but she would have recognized his voice anywhere.

* * * * *

Why did Matt Shaffer leave heiress-turned-cop Natalie Rothchild?
What does he know about the death of Natalie's twin sister?
Come and meet these two reunited lovers and learn the secrets of the Rothchild family in
THE HEIRESS'S 2-WEEK AFFAIR
by USA TODAY bestselling author Marie Ferrarella.
The first book in Silhouette® Romantic Suspense's wildly romantic new continuity,
LOVE IN 60 SECONDS!
Available April 2009.

CELEBRATE
60 YEARS
OF PURE READING PLEASURE
WITH **HARLEQUIN®**!

**Look for Silhouette®
Romantic Suspense in April!**

Love In 60 Seconds

Bright lights. Big city. Hearts in overdrive.

Silhouette® Romantic Suspense is celebrating
Harlequin's 60th Anniversary with six stories that
promise to bring readers the glitz of Las Vegas,
the danger of revenge, the mystery of a missing
diamond, and family scandals.

**Look for the first title, *The Heiress's 2-Week Affair*
by *USA TODAY* bestselling author
Marie Ferrarella, on sale in April!**

His 7-Day Fiancée by **Gail Barrett**	May
The 9-Month Bodyguard by **Cindy Dees**	June
Prince Charming for 1 Night by **Nina Bruhns**	July
Her 24-Hour Protector by **Loreth Anne White**	August
5 minutes to Marriage by **Carla Cassidy**	September

---

www.eHarlequin.com   SRS60BPA

Harlequin® Historical
Historical Romantic Adventure!

Undone!

THE RAKE'S INHERITED COURTESAN
Ann Lethbridge

Christopher Evernden has been
assigned the unfortunate task of minding
Parisian courtesan Sylvia Boisette.
When Syliva sets off to find her father,
Christopher has no choice but to follow
and finds her kidnapped by an Irishman.
Once rescued, they finally succumb to
the temptation that has been brewing
between them. But can they see past the
limitations such a love can bring?

Available April 2009
wherever books are sold.

www.eHarlequin.com

HH29541

◈ HARLEQUIN®

INTRIGUE

B.J. DANIELS

FIVE BROTHERS

ONE MARRIAGE-PACT
RACE TO THE HITCHING POST

❧ WHITEHORSE ❧
MONTANA
The Corbetts

SHOTGUN BRIDE

Available April 2009

Catch all five adventures in
this new exciting miniseries
from B.J. Daniels!

www.eHarlequin.com   HI69392

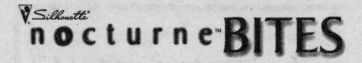

nocturne BITES

**Dark, sexy and not quite human.
Introducing a collection of
new paranormal short stories
by top Nocturne authors.**

Look for the first collection—
MIDNIGHT CRAVINGS
**Featuring Werewolf and Hellhound stories
from**
MICHELE HAUF, KAREN WHIDDON,
LORI DEVOTI, ANNA LEONARD,
VIVI ANNA **and** BONNIE VANAK.

**Indulge in Nocturne Bites
beginning in April 2009.**

Available wherever books are sold.

www.silhouettenocturne.com
www.paranormalromanceblog.wordpress.com

SNBITES09R

The Inside Romance newsletter has a NEW look for the new year!

Same great content, brand-new look!

The Inside Romance newsletter is a FREE quarterly newsletter highlighting our upcoming series releases and promotions!

Click on the Inside Romance link on the front page of **www.eHarlequin.com** or e-mail us at insideromance@harlequin.ca to sign up to receive your FREE newsletter today!

You can also subscribe by writing to us at: HARLEQUIN BOOKS Attention: Customer Service Department P.O. Box 9057, Buffalo, NY 14269-9057

Please allow 4-6 weeks for delivery of the first issue by mail.

IRNNEW09

REQUEST YOUR FREE BOOKS!

2 FREE NOVELS PLUS 2 FREE GIFTS!

SPECIAL EDITION®

Life, Love and Family!

YES! Please send me 2 FREE Silhouette Special Edition® novels and my 2 FREE gifts (gifts are worth about $10). After receiving them, if I don't wish to receive any more books, I can return the shipping statement marked "cancel." If I don't cancel, I will receive 6 brand-new novels every month and be billed just $4.24 per book in the U.S. or $4.99 per book in Canada, plus 25¢ shipping and handling per book and applicable taxes, if any*. That's a savings of at least 15% off the cover price! I understand that accepting the 2 free books and gifts places me under no obligation to buy anything. I can always return a shipment and cancel at any time. Even if I never buy another book from Silhouette, the two free books and gifts are mine to keep forever.

235 SDN EEYU   335 SDN EEY6

Name _____ (PLEASE PRINT)

Address _____ Apt. #

City _____ State/Prov. _____ Zip/Postal Code

Signature (if under 18, a parent or guardian must sign)

Mail to the **Silhouette Reader Service:**
IN U.S.A.: P.O. Box 1867, Buffalo, NY 14240-1867
IN CANADA: P.O. Box 609, Fort Erie, Ontario L2A 5X3

Not valid to current subscribers of Silhouette Special Edition books.

Want to try two free books from another line?
Call 1-800-873-8635 or visit www.morefreebooks.com.

* Terms and prices subject to change without notice. N.Y. residents add applicable sales tax. Canadian residents will be charged applicable provincial taxes and GST. Offer not valid in Quebec. This offer is limited to one order per household. All orders subject to approval. Credit or debit balances in a customer's account(s) may be offset by any other outstanding balance owed by or to the customer. Please allow 4 to 6 weeks for delivery. Offer available while quantities last.

Your Privacy: Silhouette is committed to protecting your privacy. Our Privacy Policy is available online at www.eHarlequin.com or upon request from the Reader Service. From time to time we make our lists of customers available to reputable third parties who may have a product or service of interest to you. If you would prefer we not share your name and address, please check here. ☐

SSE08R